TABBY MONROE

Radio Vamp

BLACK CHERRY
PUBLISHING

Contents

Contents

Prologue

"*L*et... me... see."

The woman snapped her fingers in front of the microphone, mouth pursed as she stared at the screen of her laptop. Her platinum blonde hair was swept to one side, braided over her shoulder, and her tight pink dress and white blazer screamed that she was from out of town.

Boiling River residents didn't wear tight dresses and heels. Clothes like that weren't practical out here in the desert valley—the stilettos would sink into the soft patches of dirt, and the dusty breeze would stain her blazer. She'd never be able to run from the sudden sinkholes which opened up under residents' feet dressed like that. And the cacti would love those bare legs, leaning over to stroke and scratch.

Besides, the outfit was showy, and it was a cardinal sin among the locals to be seen as self-important. No one was anyone in Boiling River. That was why the town was so popular with supernaturals.

The woman—what was her name again? Helen or Helena or

something—gave Zacharias a dazzling smile and sat back in her seat. They were in Crispy Biscuit, Boiling River's 24-hour diner, a temple of greased metal tables and neon signs, and Zacharias was surprised she'd consented to sit in the cracked red leather booths at all. The radio hummed in the background, drowned out in bursts by the sizzle of burgers slapped on the grill, and maybe-Helena pushed the microphone closer to him across the salt-crusted table.

"So. Zacharias."

He forced a smile. Was that supposed to be a question? Should he answer it somehow? The woman waited, eyebrows raised, then clicked her tongue and pushed on with her joke of an interview.

Zacharias fought the urge to roll his eyes and shifted in his seat, determined to listen.

"How long have you lived in Boiling River?"

That was an easy one. "Six months."

Usually, Zacharias guarded even the most minute details of his life like a dragon. But his arrival in Boiling River was a matter of public record—all supernaturals had to check in and disclose the nature of their powers—and he owed his boss this favor. Otis had taken a chance on him. Tossed him a lifeline when he didn't owe him a thing. But when Otis gave Zacharias a job on the radio, he had no idea what a hit the vampire's show would be.

Neither did Zacharias. It was all very disconcerting.

"And where did you live before?"

Zacharias shrugged one shoulder. He didn't live anywhere. Not for a long time.

"I'm from northern England originally." Again, screamingly obvious by his accent. "Came over. Spent some time in New

York. Down to Lima. La Paz. Cochabamba. Then New Orleans, Toronto, and Alaska before finding my way here."

It was a snapshot. The tip of the metaphorical iceberg. And, since he couldn't help himself, deliberately misleading. He'd been to all those places, it was true, but he'd stayed in others for far longer.

Zacharias was used to muddying his own trail. It had served him in the first years of his afterlife, haunting the shadows of London's back alleys, and it couldn't hurt now when he faced down the specter of minor fame.

He'd agreed to this favor. To interview for this woman's podcast. But he would not bare his soul to a damn microphone, nor to a strange woman who ordered a salad in a diner. A burger hissed as it hit the grill over his shoulder, and Zacharias' stomach clenched. He tugged his drink closer, jabbing the paper straw until the floating ice cream mixed with the blood.

"A desert is an unusual choice for a vampire." His interviewer leaned forward, her cleavage shadowed at the top of her dress. She used this tactic a lot. "So much sunlight. Aren't you afraid?"

Zacharias shrugged. It was true: he could go outside here less than in Toronto or Alaska, and the second he forgot himself and stepped into sunshine, he'd be burned away to ash. The wind that whistled through the valley would scatter his atoms over the cactus fields. But the draw of Boiling River wasn't the weather. It wasn't the baking hot sun and cracked earth; the warm breezes charged with static electricity.

It was community. Supernaturals could come here and live a normal life. And Zacharias must have been sloppy and sentimental one evening, because he'd come here against his best judgement and even settled down enough to get a damn job.

Pathetic, really. He'd have to move along soon. Already, people were paying him too much attention. Like this interview, for instance—he would never have agreed to such a risk elsewhere. But Otis gave him those awful puppy dog eyes, and he'd caved.

"Your show is a runaway hit. A cultural phenomenon." The woman toyed with the microphone cable, rolling it between her manicured finger and thumb. "Are you enjoying your success?"

"No." She twitched, surprised. No doubt the idea that Zacharias would rather be left alone, would rather an anonymous existence in the shadows, was utterly alien to this woman. She'd taken no less than twelve photos of them together the minute he'd walked through the door.

She was a fool. Scrutiny was a curse, and Zacharias regretted even the mild success of his show. He hadn't set out to gain fans or make waves—he simply fancied something to do in the long, lonely nights. He didn't even know why so many humans went mad for him. He just talked into a microphone and pressed buttons, then played other people's music.

Zacharias eyed the microphone pointed his way with distaste. They were nothing but trouble.

The woman's phone buzzed next to her elbow, rattling over the metal table. She held up a finger to him, tapped a key on her laptop, then snatched up her phone.

"Yelena. What is it?"

Yelena. He'd been close, Zacharias mused, sucking on his straw and drawing sweet, coppery blood down his parched throat. No matter how much he drank, he was always thirsty.

Always.

Even now, his gaze fastened on the pulse fluttering beneath Yelena's pale jaw. It was frantic, hammering against her skin, belying her calm demeanor. She may seem confident and professional, but her body told a different truth: she was sitting across from a predator, and she knew it. They both knew it. Zacharias was a bundle of vicious instincts, packaged loosely in a black cotton t-shirt and faded jeans.

Zacharias sighed and dragged his gaze away, sucking harder at his straw. This whole interview was a waste of time. Why the hell would anyone want to hear about him? He was a presenter in a tiny radio station in an end-of-the-road desert town. There were vamps out there who'd toppled empires and advised kings; who'd become captains of industry or movie stars.

Zacharias kept to himself. When he saw the great and powerful, he rolled his eyes and walked the other way. It made for a peaceful life, but for a boring interview.

"Sorry about that," Yelena breathed, placing her phone back on the table. She tapped a key on her laptop, curled her lips into a seductive smirk, and leaned closer. "Where were we?"

Zacharias shrugged and forced a strained smile.

Someone stake him now.

Chapter One

~⚬⚬~

*C*laire Ramsden did not believe in supernatural creatures. Oh, she knew they existed, alright. You couldn't spend twenty-four years in Boiling River and stay naïve about things that go bump in the night.

The little old lady next door was a banshee. Her hairdresser was fae. The day after every full moon, Claire picked up her damn trash cans from halfway down the street where they'd been tossed by rowdy werewolves.

Seriously.

Every. Damn. Month.

Supernaturals might be real, but they were also a pain in her ass. And no matter how many sappy posters and cheesy slogans about Boiling River the town council put out, Claire Ramsden sometimes wished she lived far away from here. Somewhere where supernatural creatures at least pretended to be nothing but folk tales. Somewhere where wolves didn't make a stinking wreck of her street, and charming vampires didn't seduce away little girls' mothers.

Claire yanked on a metal handle, wrinkling her nose at the stink wafting from her trash cans. She'd forgotten to check the moon last night before cooking curry, and now the remnants of her dinner were splattered over the sidewalk.

A rookie mistake. One that no Boiling River local should ever make. But Claire was distracted lately, barely remembering to cook at all. It was all piling up: unfinished paintings for clients; nursing home bills for her dad; last week's dishes in the sink. A mountain of responsibilities towered over Claire and threatened to engulf her.

It wasn't supposed to be like this. Adulthood. She was fairly sure. Claire had cringed through all those workshops in high school about going out into the world and becoming a functioning member of society. They'd told her about taxes and sexual health, but no one had warned her about the constant undercurrent of dread. And now, years later, there was soured milk in her refrigerator and her truck wouldn't start.

She wanted to ask for her time back, somehow.

The cheap metal of the trash can scraped and bounced over the cement, and Claire tugged harder, sweating through her t-shirt. A banana peel lay in her path, splayed like a murder victim and cooking in the desert sun.

Claire took a deep breath, mentally cursed all werewolves to the ninth circle of hell, and pinched the banana peel between her thumb and forefinger. It *squidged*, its insides oozing onto her skin.

"For gods' sake," she muttered, tossing the slimy peel on top of the rest of the trash and wiping her hands on her overalls. "Freaking wolves."

It was the same every month. She'd pick up her garbage, strewn across the sidewalk, and stuff it stinking back into the trash. Then, after scrubbing herself raw in the shower, she'd sit down at her laptop, crack her knuckles, and write her complaint all over again.

It never made any difference. Oh, the Boiling River town council loved to spout slogans about inter-species harmony. About how here, out in the desert and under the stars, supernatural creatures and humans had learned to get along. To live in peace as neighbors and lovers and friends, and don't forget to thank your local representatives!

Claire would thank them when they protected her damn trash cans. Until then, she sent the same email each month, received the same formal reply, then made mental plans to get out of Boiling River.

The places she'd go. The art she'd make. The functioning adult she would become.

She'd start somewhere very, very cold.

Somewhere with six-foot snowbanks, and not a supernatural in sight.

* * *

Her kitchen was blissfully cool when she stepped inside, hurrying straight to the sink to scrub at her hands. She'd shower in a moment, but first—Claire swiped her battered watering can off the window sill and held it under the faucet.

All around the kitchen, clustered on every counter and lining each shelf, were an army of plant pots. And in each pot, poking through the soil, was a small, dead plant. Crunchy brown leaves or bald, soggy stems. Claire killed them all in their own special way.

She sighed, tilting the watering can over her brand new basil plant, its pot squeezed in the center of the window sill. Right in the pool of sunshine, a breeze from the window rustling its leaves.

"Come on, little guy." The drops pattered against the soil. "Stay with me. We can do this."

Her dad loved plants. He could nurse a seedling into a shrub in record time. Claire grew up surrounded by greenery, their house an indoor jungle in the middle of the rocky sands which stretched for miles around. And when her dad moved into the Boiling River nursing home a year ago, her little oasis died off, plant by plant.

A black thumb. That's what the gnome who ran the garden superstore diagnosed her with. A chronic inability to keep the hardiest of plants alive. It wasn't neglect—she hovered over the little shoots like the worst helicopter parent. She followed instructions to the letter; spent hours researching plant ailments and proper care.

It was a mystery. Some kind of judgement from above—or below, or wherever. You never knew in Boiling River. Maybe she'd pissed off a minor deity, or offended a fairy sprite. Claire put the watering can down with a thunk, grabbed a witch-blessed pebble from a saucer, kissed it, and placed it on the soil.

"Claire-Bear?"

The voice floated through the open window, loud and shrill. Claire stifled a grin and let herself out the back door, stepping back into the blazing morning heat.

"Hey, Mabel."

Her neighbor was draped over the fence, a vision of turquoise jewelry and shawls. A pair of huge, knock-off designer sunglasses rested on her snub nose, reflecting Claire's sweaty, frazzled face back to her, and Mabel's white, dandelion hair stood out in a halo around her head.

She clucked as Claire walked closer, beaming and showing a slick of purple lipstick on her front tooth.

Claire waved.

Mabel opened her mouth and screamed.

It was the sort of sound that made your whole body flinch. A deafening, nails-on-a-chalkboard, make your teeth ache sound. Claire crossed her arms, gripped her elbows to stop from clapping her palms over her ears, and forced a polite smile as Mabel finished her scream.

It wasn't like Mabel could help it. Mabel was a banshee.

After just over a minute, the scream faded into a spluttering cough. Claire reached for her neighbor but Mabel waved her off, her chunky bracelets clinking.

"Sorry, love."

"Don't worry about it." Claire eyed the old woman leaning against her fence. She'd grown up in this house—it was the only home she'd ever known—and for all that time, Mabel had lived next door. As far back as Claire could remember, she'd heard the banshee's screams, and Mabel had always looked old enough to turn into dust.

But did she look more tired than usual? Claire gnawed on her bottom lip.

"Have you heard?" Mabel wheezed. "Have you listened?"

Claire groaned. "Spare me the mystic crap, Mabel. You know I can't tune into shit."

It was a sore spot. The Boiling River residents with powers—magic or clairvoyance, something you were born with and not turned into—presented in high school. There was no rhyme or reason to who was chosen, and the Boiling River

10

teenagers spent most spare minutes obsessing about whether they'd get lucky.

Whether they'd be special. Sensitive to something more.

Claire had held onto hope for an embarrassingly long amount of time. Long after the other human teenagers moved on with their lives. But she'd got the message eventually. She'd stopped caring and obsessing the day Dad sat her down and told her he was ill. She was plain old Claire Ramsden, and she had bigger things to worry about than magic.

Mabel rolled her eyes, the movement so exaggerated that her sunglasses rose and fell on her face.

"No? Can you tune into a radio, Claire-Bear?"

Oh. Claire frowned, nudging a rock with the toe of her sneaker. A lizard shot out and skittered across the dirt, its tail lashing behind it.

"Is it the station?"

Of course it was. There was only one radio station worth listening to in Boiling River: Supernatural Airwaves. People tuned in from miles around; they drove for hours to lay out in truck beds and stargaze as they let the radio play.

"There's a new man." Mabel's purple mouth stretched wide. "A *gentleman*."

Please. Mabel was man-crazy, that was all. When the firefighters drove past in their truck, she hung out her living room window and screamed until they turned off the street.

"I don't really…"

"Listen to him, Claire." Mabel gave a sloppy wink, her sunglasses shifting forwards. "Listen to him and thank me. His voice is *ever* so deep."

Claire cleared her throat. "Uh. Sure. Thanks, Mabel."

She waited until the little old banshee shuffled back inside, her jeweled flip flops slapping against her heels. Then she leaned against the fence, frowning out past Mabel's garden, out to the mountains beyond.

A new resident. A man on the radio. These were her life's big surprises? In a valley where water ran uphill for twenty minutes each day, and angels streaked overhead?

This couldn't be her life. Something had to give.

Chapter Two

⁕

Zacharias York stopped believing in humans decades ago.

He wasn't a fool. He'd been human once, and they were constantly, aggressively there. Everywhere he walked, he was surrounded by the faint thump of blood pulsing through veins. They stared at him, the way an antelope might stare at a lion. And when they did, their eyes went fuzzy.

For the last two hundred years or so, humans had been nothing but a disappointment. A gawping, staring, lusting, quick-to-grab-the-pitchforks disappointment.

At least in Boiling River, Zacharias didn't have to hide his fangs. He didn't have to wear contacts which made his red eyes itch, or make excuses for never going out in the day. Previously, he'd claimed to be an agoraphobe. To have rare skin conditions or life-threatening allergies. At least here, he could drop the charade.

It was one point in the desert town's favor. He wasn't so sure about the rest. Everyone in Boiling River was so damn chipper, and it set his fangs on edge.

Zacharias lowered himself into his salt water pool. This apartment was his biggest indulgence—the part of this town he'd be most sad to leave. An underground lair, the apartment was worthy of any Hollywood villain; the cavernous space was cut into the rock and filled with every possible diversion.

A huge cinema screen. A swimming pool. Floor to ceiling bookshelves and a small but well stocked laboratory.

What could he say? He'd been alive for two hundred years and never slept. Zacharias got bored. And he snagged it cheap from the last vamp who lived here, who'd left Boiling River in a hurry.

Illegal? Probably. Suspicious? Definitely. But it was none of Zacharias' business.

The water was cold, the sensations registering dimly, but since he had no body heat it hardly mattered. His arms cut through the water, propelling him from one end to the other, and Zacharias counted off lengths in his head.

He counted in Japanese. Swahili. Romanian. Elvish. Orc-tongue.

It didn't help. Zacharias was bored out of his skull.

The water cascaded down his body as Zacharias pushed out of the pool, his skin pale and unflushed despite the workout. It still freaked him out to see that part, even after all these years. Back before he'd turned, he'd worked in the mines, his skin blushing and slick with sweat.

He grabbed a towel off a lounger and rubbed himself dry, keeping his eyes firmly away from his torso.

A glance at the clock showed 5pm. Gods, this day was endless. When his phone chirped from a lounger, he snatched it up with embarrassing speed.

Otis: Drinks before work?? Silver Bullet, next to the emporium

Otis: Bring ur smile :) :) :)

Sarcastic ass. Zacharias rolled his eyes and tossed his phone back to the lounger without replying.

His werewolf boss. And a grimy bar in a two-bit desert town. Was this what it had come to? He may work with the overgrown dog, but he didn't have to socialize.

Zacharias stalked to the nearest bookcase, running a finger along the spines. There was everything here, from old tomes bound in vellum to the latest airport thriller. He could read, he supposed, or watch old horror films, or get back into the pool for another swim…

He typed out the reply before he could overthink it, screwing one eye shut as his fingers blurred over his phone screen.

Zacharias: I'll be there.

Otis: Hell yeah, bloodsucker!

Zacharias pinched the bridge of his nose, cursing his own foolishness. This would be nothing short of hellish, and then he had a whole night shift with the great hairy oaf. Was it not enough that they spent hours together, cooped up in recording booths?

This was what happened when he let his mind wander. When he didn't have a research project or something to focus on. He grew pathetic and lonely, subjecting himself to the company of idiots to keep the boredom away. Zacharias huffed, disgusted with himself, and slung his towel around his shoulders.

Too late to back out now. Time to go and teach himself a lesson.

* * *

Otis was loud. And not just at the full moon; he was loud when he greeted Zacharias in the street, clapping him on the shoulder and laughing up at the darkening sky. He was loud when they ducked inside the Silver Bullet, yelling in Zacharias' ear about playing pool or finding a table. And he was deafening as he ordered a drink, booming to the bartender about a whisky sour.

Zacharias closed his eyes and settled his shoulders. Forced blankness to fill his thoughts. It was just one drink. One evening. He could do this.

"What are you having?"

Otis gripped his shoulder and shook, and Zacharias shrugged the hand off, bristling. A sharp, brown-haired woman eyed them from behind the bar, her plump mouth twisting as she poured Otis his drink.

"Bloody Mary," Zacharias bit out. "O negative."

The bartender's eyebrow twitched, but she said nothing. She slid Otis his whisky and turned to open a fridge, the rows of crimson blood in glass bottles clinking together.

Zacharias couldn't help it. He sucked in a breath, the gust of cool, coppery air washing over him despite the sealed bottles.

He was a vampire, and he was old. He could scent blood like a shark; on the other side of the bar, there was a woman with a day-old paper cut that was giving him a headache. His fangs grew, pricking at his bottom lip, and his stomach growled loud enough to hear over the jukebox.

Otis roared with laughter, and the woman glanced back over her shoulder, her gaze landing on his sharp teeth.

Zacharias pressed his lips together and scowled. This gods-damned werewolf.

"I've got this," Zacharias muttered, but Otis slapped cash

16

down on the bar and herded him away. Zacharias swiped for his drink, lifting it to his lips and trying not to suck it down like a desperate junkie. He timed his sips, counting to ten between each lift of the glass, and tried valiantly to ignore the automatic swelling in his dark jeans.

"My mother used to love a Bloody Mary." Otis paused by a standing table, resting one elbow on the wood. It groaned under the weight of his muscled arm. "The tomato kind, though." He winked. "Not the bloodsuckers' kind. She drank them on Wednesday nights when her lady friends came over to play bridge."

Zacharias could feel the question coming, bearing down on him like an eighteen-wheeler down the highway.

"Your mom like cocktails, Zach?"

"My mother is dead," Zacharias said stiffly. "And it's Zacharias."

Otis hummed and sipped his whisky, hissing through his teeth. "What did your mom like, then?"

It was not an outlandish question, even if it were extremely nosy. It was the sort of question Zacharias should know the answer to. And he must have known, once upon a time. He must have known more details of his mother beyond the flashes left in his memory—her crocheting by the fire; her kneading dough with cracked knuckles; her gravelly laugh when his father cracked a joke.

"Us," he said shortly. "She liked us. My brothers and sisters, and my father most of all."

Otis snorted. "Well, yeah. I figured she'd like you. That's practically the law. What did she like that she wasn't supposed to?"

Zacharias scowled at the scratched wood of the table. He

17

remembered her laugh so clearly, and it was the laugh of a woman who knew the world. But whatever she thought of it, whatever her secret vices, she'd never shared them with her son.

"Cigars." He eyed the gnome puffing away outside the bar window. It was as good as any lie. "She swiped cigars from my father's stash and smoked them out by the laundry."

Otis raised his glass, clinking it against Zacharias' drink before knocking it back. "What a woman."

Indeed.

A flash of platinum blonde hair caught his eye, and Zacharias nodded reluctantly to the woman a few tables away. It was Yelena, the podcaster he'd bored with his desperately dull afterlife. Yelena lifted a hand, her smile sheepish as she half-listened to the gnome talking into her microphone. Apparently she wasn't done with Boiling River. He'd failed to scare her away.

This was a mistake. Coming to this bar, ordering this drink—hell, moving to this desert valley six months ago—it was all an exercise in humiliation.

Zacharias didn't know what he was thinking. Perhaps he was finally going senile.

"Pool!" Otis boomed, sending the two gangly men currently playing hurrying back to the bar. The balls clinked against the edge of the table, their cues left abandoned on the felt.

"Alright." Zacharias took a gulp of his drunk and winced as his cock twitched. It was instinct, a reflex to the blood, but it had gotten him in trouble before. The gods knew the last thing he needed was this wolf misreading his situation for genuine interest. He'd bedded a female werewolf once, back in the 1920s, and it had taken months to get that dog smell out of his sofa.

No; Zacharias had learned a long time ago—back when he was human, even—that relationships were not for him.

He preferred to be free. Solitary. Unfettered. Beholden to no one and nothing.

Even moving to a town like this—a town where people knew him, knew what he was—made his skin prickle with unease. And agreeing to work nights in the radio station... well, that had been nothing short of madness.

He kept telling himself he'd quit. Especially after the first packet of fan mail arrived at the station. There were stories in there, so rude they would once have brought color to his cheeks. There were drawings, too, though of course the listeners had no idea what he truly looked like.

Apparently they pictured him with washboard abs and a billowing pirate's shirt... if the drawings had any clothes at all. Otis roared with laughter whenever he caught sight of one; he'd snagged the most ridiculous drawing and hung it framed in the Supernatural Airwaves staff room.

So he'd sworn he'd quit, striding around his cavernous apartment and raking his hands through his hair. But then the boredom would set in again, and he found himself back in that radio booth. No matter the letters. No matter that damn podcast interview. No matter the trapped, panicked feeling that hit him at odd hours.

Soon. He'd quit soon. He'd leave the station behind and never have to see this deafening werewolf again. And Zacharias would cut all ties, pack up his Bond villain lair, and get out of this desert town.

Chapter Three

" *H* oly shit."

Claire cranked the volume on the bar's dusty old radio, turning her head so she could hear better. Her red hair spilled over her shoulders, and she strained to listen to the crackling connection. Bree dropped the pizza box onto the table and threw herself into the chair opposite.

They were in the Silver Bullet's back room, a half hour after closing. Claire and her quiet friend Olivia had trooped in as the bell rang for last orders, ready to wipe down tables for twenty minutes then eat pizza in the back and gossip. Bree, the prickly but beautiful bartender, summoned them more nights than not, and both Claire and Olivia went without complaint.

Claire was an artist. A painter. It didn't matter what time she went to bed. Her house was so quiet, now, without Dad, and she could use the distraction.

And poor Olivia was an insomniac and grateful for the company after dark.

It worked between them. It had since school, when all three

had sighed with private relief that if they were plain human, at least they were human together. Bree was the spitfire, Olivia the sweetheart, and Claire the voice of reason.

And right now, the voice of reason needed the others to shut the hell up.

"Listen," she hissed, dialing the volume up to full. A deep, husky voice filled the room, reverberating the glasses on the table.

It was a dark voice. Dripping with the promise of sin. Claire's eyes screwed shut, her toes curling in her sneakers as she squeezed her thighs together.

They listened, spellbound, while the voice spoke. The words weren't important—Claire barely registered what he was saying. All that mattered was that he kept talking. His accent sounded British, but not the polished, stuffy kind. He sounded rough and sturdy.

There was a growl in his throat. A smokiness to his tone. It was the sort of voice that promised to put you over its knee.

A song faded in, bluesy and pulsing, and all three of them sat back and stared at the crappy radio.

"Holy shit," Bree said flatly.

Olivia squeaked.

Claire swallowed, her throat suddenly dry, and swiped for her bottle of cider.

Ever so deep, Mabel had said, lounging over their garden fence. Well, she wasn't wrong. Claire's pulse thudded in her throat.

"That's got to be a vamp." Bree kicked her ankle boots up on a spare chair. She levered the pizza box open, and the smell of oregano and melted cheese wafted through the room. Bree tore off a slice, folded it in half, and stuffed most of it into her mouth in one go. Crumbs and flecks of flour dropped onto her black top, and she brushed them away, unconcerned.

"I saw a new vamp earlier," she said through a mouthful of pizza dough. Claire wrinkled her nose. Olivia's hand snaked towards the box, tugging it closer to the center of the table. "He came in with that werewolf jackass who runs the radio station. The one who won't shut the hell up. *Whisky sour.* Please."

Claire tore off her own slice and took a bite to avoid saying anything. Bree and Olivia seemed fine—a little dazed, maybe—but Claire's nerves were jangling inside her. She crossed her ankles under her chair, practically crawling out of her skin.

Who the hell was that? And why did Claire feel like she'd just stuck her finger in an outlet?

She'd met vampires before; everyone in Boiling River had. Hell, there were vamps on that damn town council. And even though a few of the Boiling River vamps had tried that glamor shit on her, it had never worked before.

You had to be amenable, see. Open to their influence. And if one thing was certain about Claire Ramsden, it was that she would never let a vampire in.

Not willingly, anyway. She scowled at the radio.

"What was he like?" she heard herself ask, her voice distant.

Bree hummed, licking tomato sauce off her thumb as she considered.

"Stern," she said at last. "Not fancy like most of the vamps. Kind of gruff. And like he'd rather be anywhere but here."

Claire rolled that thought around her mind, thinking idly of her travel mood board. The one propped up in her living room, covered in cut out scraps from magazines.

Places she'd go one day, when she'd earned enough from her paintings to see more of the world than Boiling River. Ways she'd make her life remarkable, no matter how human she remained.

So what was a stuck-up British vamp doing here? And why was her skin still tingling, the little hairs on her arms standing on end?

Claire bit into her pizza, her forehead set in a frown.

No. This guy was bad news. And with any luck, she'd never hear his voice again.

* * *

The kitchen was silent and eerie when Claire let herself in the back door. It was force of habit, tramping all the way around the bungalow to come through the kitchen. She'd started as a teenager, just after her mom left and the house seemed to yawn wide open with emptiness. Before, when Claire came home from school, her mom would be sat at her sewing table in the living room, stitching and mending. The rattle of that sewing machine was how Claire knew she was home.

Then her mom upped and left, lured away by honeyed whispers of a passing vampire. She was so dazzled by the unearthly man, she didn't even take her things. Just a single, small suitcase, with a week's worth of clothes and her battered old hairdryer.

And Claire and her father were left behind in their bungalow, both avoiding the living room until Dad snapped and called a moving company to collect the abandoned sewing machine.

It seemed silly now that Claire had thought the house was cold and empty when her mother left. Now it really *was* just her, with her graveyard of dead plants and a leaky faucet. The water *drip-dripped* into the kitchen sink, and Claire sighed and wrenched at the handle as she walked past.

Drip. Drip.

Screw. You.

Moonlight spilled through the large kitchen windows, bathing her basil plant in silvery light and casting weird shadows over the surfaces. The blessed pebble she'd placed on the soil hummed quietly, the only sound except the dripping water and the *tick-tock* of the clock on the wall.

1:30am. Hours past when a proper, responsible adult would be in bed. Claire gnawed on her bottom lip, tugging the refrigerator door and fishing out a beer.

Just one more drink. To calm her buzzing nerves. She was still antsy, her skin hypersensitive to every breeze and brush of fabric. When she screwed off the bottle cap and leaned back against the counter, she could feel every shift of her t-shirt against her stomach. Every seam of her jeans on her legs. The ridge of the counter dug into her spine, and Claire took a long pull on the bottle, gazing out the window across the desert.

That damn vampire. He had no gods-damn right to make her feel this way.

And yet...

The problem with living alone was there was no one watching her. No one to keep her in check, even unknowingly. The gods knew her dad was about as strict as a puppy, but even knowing he was a few rooms over was enough to keep her teenage urges tamped down.

Dad was gone. Streets away. And though Claire was twenty-four now, she still had her fair share of reckless impulses.

Especially tonight. That damn vampire. Claire groaned, the sound bouncing off her cupboards.

She didn't have a radio. She'd bought a shitty shower radio

once in her retro phase, but it hung forgotten in the bathroom, colonized by spiders. Which meant she couldn't just flick a switch and pretend to herself it was a casual gesture. No, she had to hunt her laptop down in the sofa cushions and plug in the charger, booting up the cracked screen. She had to wait for the dodgy internet to connect, then navigate to the Supernatural Airwaves website.

By the time Claire clicked on the button to tune in live, she was filled to the eyebrows with self-loathing.

A song was playing. It was edgy, experimental—all techno effects and unrecognizable instruments. Oh yeah, this guy was a vamp alright. They were all pretentious as hell. Claire listened to the song play through, her nose wrinkled in disdain and her knee bouncing where she sat on the sofa.

Gods. What was she doing? A vampire? Really? Claire huffed, shifting forward and reaching for the laptop. She'd slam it shut, delete the site from her browser history, and tell herself this never happened.

But just as her fingertips curled over the laptop's edge, the song faded away. It faded, and *he* came back, speaking quiet and low like he was talking directly into her ear. Like he'd brushed her hair to the side and put his lips right to her earlobe.

"… Here's one for the night-time supernaturals, and the humans that just can't sleep…"

Claire shivered, squirming on the lumpy sofa. Moonlight shone through the windows here too, casting silvery shafts of light across the stone tiles. It washed over where she sat, over where her chest heaved and her nipples pebbled against her t-shirt. Claire listened to the man speak, gasping for breath, her ears ringing and her thoughts screaming. And when she finally worked up the will to slam the laptop shut, her hand straining towards the screen like she was pushing through butter, she sat in the sudden silence and listened to her thundering heart.

It was… a joke. It was *bullshit*, she raged inwardly, cringing as she shifted and felt the dampness between her legs. Humiliation stained her cheeks, even with no one here to see it.

Claire knew it. She felt the traitorous clench low in her abdomen. She felt the way her skin flushed hot all over.

First her damn trash cans for the fifth month in a row, tossed around by freaking werewolves, and now *this*. Glamored by a vampire in her own home.

Bullshit.

The town council would listen to her this time. She would make sure of it.

Chapter Four

*T*wo nights later, Zacharias sat in the cramped office he shared with the local cupid and stared at the teetering pile of fan mail on his desk.

It was getting ridiculous. It must be a prank or something. These people couldn't even see him, and yet here they were, declaring their undying love and searing passions. They promised him their blood; their bodies; their hands in marriage. They offered him small fortunes in return for one night, so long as they could do anything they wanted to him.

Zacharias rolled his eyes. He didn't live past two hundred years old because he trusted strangers.

He flicked through the letters, noting the anatomy of some drawings. Not only did these people have the temerity to draw him nude, they vastly underestimated the size of his package.

It was insulting. And it was becoming a nightly nuisance. It wasn't just the fan mail—it was the clusters of people who had begun to wait for him on the sidewalk outside the station before his shifts. They begged for his autograph and pressed themselves against his arm as he reluctantly signed their scraps of paper.

One letter on his desk caught his eye—and how could it not, when it was bathed in pink glitter? Its author had sprayed the paper with perfume, and the cloying scent stung in his nose.

He recognized that handwriting. His eyes flicked to the wastepaper basket by the door.

Zacharias had been tossing all his fan mail each night, his only emotion a faint guilt at not recycling. But if he took these down the hall to the recycling cans, everyone would *see*.

No. This was a private humiliation.

And so he'd stuffed each night's packet into his office waste paper basket, the station's cupid only raising her eyebrows and mercifully saying nothing. After eight days at the station, he'd smuggled in a larger trash can.

It was getting ridiculous.

"Hello again," Zacharias murmured, teasing the pink, glittery abomination away from the stack. His instincts clamored inside him, screaming for attention—*beware, beware, beware.* His desk chair bumped over the faded grey carpet as he wheeled closer to the wastepaper basket.

There: below a scrunched up memo and a flier for a local takeout. Another pink, glitter-bombed letter.

He should have noticed before. Now that he'd seen the pattern, he recalled a similar letter each night since his first week on the job. They'd begun with neater handwriting, he suspected. And fewer threats.

Tonight's was a classic. *Marry me, bite me, make me scream. I'm eternally yours.*

"No, thank you," Zacharias muttered, then tossed the letter along with the rest of the stack into the wastepaper basket.

Honestly, these humans. They should be ashamed of themselves.

A rap on the door made him jolt back in his chair, the plastic squeaking. Otis grinned from the doorway, scratching at his short, curly beard.

"'Sup Zachary?"

"It's Zacharias."

"What's. *Up?*"

In a simpler world, one where vampires and werewolves were still mortal enemies, Zacharias could tear the burly idiot's smirking head off his shoulders and be done with this nonsense. Instead, he forced his hands to unclench from his chair and raised his eyebrows politely.

"Nothing, wolf."

Otis snorted and pushed off the door frame, crowding closer into the tiny office. There was barely enough space for two desks and chairs in here—barely enough space for two *normal* sized supernaturals. The cupid had mercifully gone in search of coffee, but there was still no room for a great hulking werewolf.

"Can I help you with something?" Zacharias asked stiffly as Otis sat on the cupid's desk. Her collection of bobble heads nodded frantically, and the wooden desk groaned in warning.

Otis hummed. "Let's hope so. We received a complaint today."

Gods send him patience to deal with these slow-witted locals. Zacharias drummed on his mouse pad.

"And?"

It was not his problem how the rest of the shows on the station performed. Oh, he may work here, may even enjoy the job more than he'd thought he would, but Zacharias didn't *care*. He never made such a rookie mistake.

The werewolf leaned down, crossing his arms over his chest. His brown skin made Zacharias look downright sallow. The tips of his canines were pointed, and his amber eyes shone as his mouth quirked up.

"*And,* new boy, the complaint is about you. About your show."

Zacharias bristled, straightening in his chair. His show? There was nothing wrong with his show—it was excellent, according to his gushing fan mail.

"The town council has sent a cease and desist," Otis continued, tossing an opened envelope onto the desk. "One of the humans complained, apparently. She says your use of glamor goes against Boiling River rules."

Glamor? He didn't use glamor. He hadn't used that particular power in years. There was no one he remotely wanted to impress, so he hadn't bothered.

This woman was an idiot. And more than that, she was an idiot who was trying to besmirch his name. Zacharias snatched up the envelope and slid out the letter. The words blurred together as he read, the paper trembling from his irritation.

When he glared up at Otis, the man was still talking. Muttering to himself about trash cans and boisterous pups.

"I don't use glamor," Zacharias said, each word slow and firm. "This is nonsense. Slander."

Otis shrugged, suddenly cheery, and lunged to his feet. The desk groaned and lurched to the side, its legs bowed.

"Sweet. I'll let them know. You can go back to reading your love letters."

Zacharias spluttered, but Otis winked and disappeared back into the hall. His boots thudded against the carpet, echoing back until a distant door banged open.

Zacharias gusted out a breath and slumped in his chair. The

letter lay on the desk, crisp, white and accusing.

Claire Ramsden. That was the complainant's name. The woman who wanted to shut down his show. If she had her way, he'd lose the only job that had interested him in thirty years.

Claire Ramsden. She couldn't be too hard to find.

* * *

Boiling River was no place to be anonymous. The town nestled in a desert valley, mountains rising on all sides, and you could stand on the top floor of the tallest building downtown and see all the way to the farthest buildings. Most of the humans had lived here their whole lives, and when supernaturals came, they tended to stay.

It took three casual questions in the radio station canteen to discover his quarry. Claire Ramsden lived on the northern outskirts, in a cluster of bungalows near the river's edge. It was close enough that Zacharias left his car in the station's underground garage, striding down Main Street under the inky night sky.

Colored lights danced overhead, similar to the aurora Zacharias had watched once at the North Pole. But these weren't polar lights; they were ribbons of magic, twisting and writhing in the night sky before settling over the mountains to sleep.

It was beautiful, Zacharias supposed. Haunting, really, if you were into that sort of thing.

But it was difficult to appreciate the unearthly beauty of Boiling River when he was spitting mad. Zacharias ground his fangs, hands curled into fists and thrust into his pockets as he strode down the empty street. A few blocks over, the clangs of upended trash cans floated into the air, followed by the outraged screech of a cat.

Glamor. She'd accused him of using his glamor. Of trying to seduce anyone and everyone who listened to his radio show. Like he was some kind of desperate creep.

Zacharias York did not need his glamor to seduce people. He was not so pathetic; so free with his charms.

Claire Ramsden would see. Oh, she would see.

The streets passed quickly, almost blurring as he stormed down the sidewalks. And all too soon, the hotels and shops of the town center turned to apartments, then houses, then bungalows. The buildings spread out and sprouted gardens, and the cars and trucks parked on the driveways grew shabbier and coated in dust.

Claire Ramsden's bungalow was unremarkable. A squat but cozy adobe home with painted blue window frames. Window boxes lined the sills, filled with baked soil and dead stems, and a shovel lay abandoned by the front path. Zacharias breathed in deeply, inhaling the scent of the woman inside.

Oh. *Oh*. Zacharias swallowed hard, willing his sudden and vicious thirst to subside. Claire Ramsden smelled sinfully good, her scent a heady mix of basil, tangerine, and turpentine. Zacharias turned his head, sucking down mouthfuls of the desert breeze, but it was no use. Her scent was everywhere, trailing down the front path and clinging to every inch of the building.

Not the front door, though, Zacharias noted with interest. He strolled down the front path, stepping over a dropped gardening glove and breathing stubbornly through his mouth.

Her scent led around the side of the bungalow, through a wooden garden gate.

It wouldn't hurt to look. To scope out his slanderer's property. Knowledge was power, after all, and Zacharias would put this Claire Ramsden in her place, regardless of how mouthwatering she smelled.

Although… it was almost overwhelming, the way her scent grew stronger the closer he walked. His fangs pricked insistently at his lip. Zacharias buried his nose in his elbow, breathing in the sleeve of his long-sleeved shirt. There: faint strains of the werewolf's scent still clung to his clothes.

At any other time, Zacharias would wrinkle his nose in distaste at Otis' scent clinging to him.. Tonight, he gritted his teeth and breathed in deep, willing the desire surging through his blood to dull.

Perfect. Who knew Otis could be so useful? Zacharias smirked to himself in the darkness, pressing his sleeve firmly against his nose as he nudged at the garden gate. It swung wide open, creaking on its hinges. This Claire woman hadn't even set the bolt. So trusting, Zacharias mused with disapproval. All the Boiling River locals were damned fools.

The rear garden was more inviting than the front. Rather than bare dirt and abandoned gardening tools, the modest space was filled with rock gardens and cacti, their rich shades of green each different from the last. A lizard's tail poked out from under one rock, and the path was inlaid with mosaic tiles.

Beautiful. Zacharias squatted, brushing the fingertips of his free hand over the tiles. Bursts of red and orange and turquoise in the middle of this dusty desert.

Claire Ramsden's back door was set with frosted glass, the reflection of the room inside warped and jumbled. It was a kitchen, Zacharias decided, when he risked a sniff. A kitchen filled with old dishes and yet more dead plants. This Claire Ramsden was a slattern, then. A judgemental slob. The worst people always were such hypocrites, casting accusations when their own affairs were a mess.

The envelope crinkled as Zacharias pulled it out of his back pocket. He held his breath as he dug in his jeans for a pen, pressing the envelope against the glass door. He didn't need to breathe, of course, but it was much more comfortable, and the prickling in his lungs was always such a tiresome reminder that he was dead.

Better that depressing reminder, though, than a lungful of Claire Ramsden's sweet scent.

His note was short. Perfunctory. His grammar was aggressively correct. Zacharias smirked to himself as he signed with a flourish, bending to slide the note under the kitchen door.

It was not often that he was able to nurse a good grudge. With any luck, Claire Ramsden would be a worthy opponent.

Chapter Five

*T*he radio station door stuck on its hinges, screeching as Claire shoved it open. It dragged over the beat-up carpet, catching on ancient scuff marks, and Claire forced it just wide enough then slipped through the gap.

Damn supernaturals. No wonder they let their front door rust shut when they were harboring freaking stalkers.

That vamp. That *asshole*. He'd been to her bungalow, he'd-he'd told her to *wash her dishes*. What else had he smelled, snooping around her house? And did he even stay outside? Or did he stalk through her private rooms, sniffing and judging and being a complete dick?

Claire blew her hair off her forehead, her hands shaking with rage. She'd known something was off the second she stepped into her kitchen this morning. The air had been wrong, practically shivering with anticipation, and her basil plant had turned away from the window to stare at the white paper on her floor.

Bastard. Claire ran her palms down the front of her paint-splattered overalls—damn it, she'd been so worked up, she forgot to change—and glared around the radio station lobby.

It was a dump. For such a judgemental ass, the vamp apparently had no qualms about working in a derelict old heap. The radio station headquarters were fourth-hand at least; the building had been a games arcade, then a Thai restaurant, then a backpacker's hostel, all in the last ten years. Supernatural Airwaves moved in eight months ago—a monumental occasion which starred on the front page of the Boiling River Gazette.

Claire shook her head and crossed to the crowded message board, scanning for directions. But the message board was as chaotic as everything else here, the papers faded and torn against the cork.

They'd have been better off blowing the building to the clouds, then starting over in the crater. Cracks spider-webbed across the adobe walls; the carpets were worn and balding; and so much grime coated the windows that less sunlight penetrated the glass than in an algae-coated fish tank. Claire whirled away from the message board and stomped off in search of a real-life person she could yell at.

For a busy radio station, there was barely anyone around. The halls were empty except for a bristly gnome pushing a cleaning trolley, earbuds wedged deep in his ears. Vending machines lined the halls, crammed with supernatural treats—cartons of blood with tiny straws attached, and packs of what looked suspiciously like dog kibble.

"Hello?" Claire's voice echoed down the hall. A sign hung from the ceiling, flickering red. It said: *On Air.*

Claire tugged her sleeve up, checking Dad's old watch on her wrist. Perfect. Her stalker's show had begun. That meant the bastard was here somewhere, and if she interrupted his stupid, seductive monologue, even better.

When she first saw his note this morning, she'd snatched it up, crammed her feet into the rubber boots abandoned by the door, and marched outside. She'd gotten halfway down the street before she remembered the guy was a vampire.

He worked at night. He wouldn't be there if she went marauding through the radio station now. And she wanted him there. Oh, yeah. She wanted to look this creep in the eye before she tore him down to size.

So Claire had stuffed her anger back inside her chest, whirling back around to her bungalow. And she'd wasted a whole day of work, knocking palettes of paint and jars of turpentine off every surface as she stomped around, clumsy with rage.

He was here now, though. Mister Deep and Husky himself. And he'd answer for the violation of her privacy.

Cease and desist, yourself, madam, he'd written. *I cannot help your weak, primal urges, and you will regret this unjust pursuit.*

Bullshit. Complete bullshit. There was no way he wasn't using his glamor. Claire had resisted dozens of vampires before she'd heard him speak, and that was with the full force of their physical presence. Their enticing scent, light and masculine; their inhuman beauty and shocking red eyes.

Claire Ramsden would not be made a fool of. Not to the damn town council, who still hadn't warned the werewolves away from her freaking trash cans. And not after the way her mom left.

She came to a halt in front of a nondescript door, a red bulb glowing above the frame. Claire sucked in one deep, steadying breath and forced her scattered brain to focus.

The door rattled in its frame as she thumped on the wood,

its pinned poster of a local band flapping. In the room beyond, the faint strains of blues music hummed.

"Stalker!" Claire yelled. "Vampire! I know you're in there, you bastard."

She didn't know, exactly, but it was a fair guess. Especially when a weird hush fell in the room, as though someone inside were holding their breath. The music played on, and Claire glared at the shut door, wishing fervently for a shifter's strength so that she could tear it straight off its hinges.

Instead, she tried the handle. It turned easily in her hand. Ironic, really, she thought distantly as she pushed the door wide open. He'd wandered past her garden gate and snooped through the windows at her kitchen, but didn't lock his own door.

The man in the recording booth stared at her, anger rippling off him in waves. The room wasn't an office; it was set up to record, with huge electronic boards of mysterious lights, dials and buttons, and a glass wall shutting the sound inside. Claire stepped through the doorway, her fists clenched at her sides, and scowled at the vampire who'd followed her home.

It was him. The song played on—the man hadn't spoken—but she'd bet her paltry life savings that this was him. She knew it as sure as she knew her own reflection. It was like recognizing an acquaintance in a dream; someone you knew a long time ago, but see again years later in perfect detail in your mind.

"You bastard," Claire growled, holding up the vampire's note. His telltale red eyes flicked to the paper in her hand, and his forehead creased. Then his gaze fell back on her and he sat back in his chair, lounging and irreverent.

A graceful twist of his fingers on a dial, and a speaker on the wall crackled to life.

"I'm afraid you are lost, madam," he drawled. Goosebumps pimpled over Claire's skin. She huffed, stepping closer to the glass and squaring her shoulders. The paper shook in her hand as she slammed it against the divider.

"Were you lost when you slid this under my door? When you stalked me like a freaking creep?"

The man frowned, clearly disgruntled, and it was the first crack in his calm expression. Claire chased that weakness, pressing so close to the glass that her breath fogged the surface.

It was just as well. The blurriness could only help with this asshole's… effect on her. Even barely speaking, sat behind a glass divider, he'd set her heart pounding in her chest. Her stomach swooped, like she'd gone over the drop on a roller coaster and left her gut behind.

Damn him. Damn him, damn him. Her skin flushed hot beneath her overalls.

He didn't look like she'd expected, though now that she saw him in person he was a perfect match to that voice. His dark hair was long and wavy, tied at the back of his neck, though curling strands escaped and fell around his face. His sharp jaw was coated in stubble—the kind that would rasp under her palm. His thick, heavy eyebrows seemed permanently lowered, and he watched her with quick, canny eyes.

Claire swallowed hard, her eyes dropping to what she could see of the rest of him. He wore a black, long-sleeved t-shirt rather than the pressed button-downs favored by most vamps, and the back of his hand was scarred where it wrapped around a chipped mug.

"You had no right," Claire croaked, forcing her thoughts back on task. "No right to use your glamor, and no right to come to my home."

"I do not use my glamor." The vampire's chair creaked as he sat forward. The song humming in the background faded away, and for a moment there was nothing. The room was silent except for the quick gasps of Claire's breaths, and the pop of static on the airwaves. The man jolted, as though remembering where he was, and he slapped quickly at the buttons until a cheery, jangling song burst into the room.

He winced, flicking an annoyed glance at the speakers, then turned the force of that stare back on Claire.

"I do not use my glamor," he said again. "Any… impact you have experienced from listening to the show is purely coincidental." Claire scoffed, but the man's mouth twisted into the ghost of a cruel smile. "Might I suggest another channel? If you are so easily affected."

That smile deepened as Claire sucked in a shocked breath, swaying with the force of her anger. This-this *asshole*, this smug, rude, sanctimonious asshole—

Her fingernails bit into her palms. The sting of pain centered Claire; brought her back down to the grubby carpet. And the vampire's nostrils flared, she noted bitterly, his form stiffening in his chair.

Good. She shouldn't be the only one so ruffled by someone she loathed. Claire squeezed her fists tighter, cutting deeper into her palms, and smirked as the vampire let out a grunt. He gripped the mug so tight, she was surprised the china wasn't pulverized into dust.

"Careful," she murmured, raising a hand as though to wave goodbye. Then, on a whim, she pressed her palm against the glass, smearing a tiny smudge of her blood. "Perhaps you should keep away from humans? If you're so easily affected."

His lip curled, the pearly white tip of a fang poking out, and

Claire tossed his note to the floor then spun around. Her pulse hammered in her throat all the way down the hallway and back through the lobby.

It hadn't gone as she'd planned, the weight of those eyes on her scattering her thoughts, but she'd done it. She'd confronted the husky-voiced vampire.

Claire's sneakers hit the sidewalk and turned directly towards the Silver Bullet.

She needed a good long drink after this. With ice—a whole bucket of ice.

* * *

"You have got to be kidding me," Claire wailed, slumping over the bar. Bree raised an eyebrow at her, bending to unload the dishwasher. "His show? Really? Turn that shit off, Bree!"

The Silver Bullet was crammed full, half with locals and half with a UFO-spotting tour group passing through in the valley. The visitors were all dressed in matching t-shirts with pictures of little green men in cowboy hats sipping cocktails.

"Sorry, girl." The smirk on Bree's crimson lips did not seem sorry. "The tourists love the radio. They come miles out of their way just to tune in."

Sure enough, they clustered in groups around the speakers, beaming at each other and listening avidly. And that bastard spoke, his smoky voice curling its hook in Claire's gut, making her aching and breathless and pissed off. She jabbed at the ice and lime in her glass, stabbing it with her straw.

"This can't be my life now. I can't spend the rest of my days unwillingly panting after that jackass."

"So get it out of your system." Bree shrugged and flicked a

dish towel over her shoulder. "You know: wham, bam, thank you vamp."

"Never." Claire was hoarse but determined. She twirled her glass on the bar, glaring at the beads of condensation. "I will never touch that man."

Bree hummed, unconvinced. The fiery bartender had no issues with scratching an itch. Plenty of times, she'd slid her phone number to someone who'd gotten her all hot and bothered—human or otherwise.

Claire had never done that. She'd never had the balls. Or ovaries, or whatever. Oh, she'd had boyfriends, sure, but she'd never hooked up.

It did sound pretty fun.

Not with him, though. She never wanted that condescending gaze on her again. And besides, a voice whispered in her head, he clearly wasn't interested, anyway.

It was so unfair. Such a slap in the face, when his mere voice made her nerves sing to life. And he had the audacity to say she was *easily affected*. To imply that it was all her, and no doing of his.

But then...

No one else was shifting on their bar stools, practically whimpering from the ache between their legs. None of the men were hiding their crotches; none of the women had flushed cheeks and bright eyes.

Maybe it was her. Was she doing this on purpose, somehow? Latching onto his voice?

Claire tossed back the dregs of her drink, the ice sliding in her glass, and waved at Bree for another.

Get it out of her system. She could do that.

But not with him. Never with him.

Chapter Six

◈

*H*er blood was overwhelming. Just that tiny smear on the glass divider, dried for hours now—Zacharias was achingly hard, and angrier than he'd been in years.

How dare she? That foolish woman had no right. It was an insult, an assault on his senses, to deliberately torment him like this. To wind him up and leave him sat here, shaking with need and thirst, while he forced himself through the rest of his shift.

Claire Ramsden was a monster.

A copper-haired, paint-splattered monster, with a constellation of freckles dusting her face. Her green eyes had dilated at the first glimpse of him, her pulse thudding against the skin of her throat like it was trying to beat its way out to him.

And she'd been so pissed off to want him like that. To be so publicly, undeniably turned on. It was his only consolation—that he wasn't alone in his humiliation. That she craved him in return.

Except.. no. Zacharias rubbed his thumb over the handle

of his mug, eyeing the clock on the wall. It counted down the minutes until he could leave this booth and get away from the torment of her blood. No, it wasn't the same. His was a natural hunger, an indiscriminate craving for blood.

It had nothing to do with Claire Ramsden. Not as a *person*.

The second hand quivered on the clock face before ticking down another minute. This entire night had been hellish, and Zacharias wanted nothing more than to surge through the streets in his tinted car and throw himself bodily in his salt water pool. He'd gorge on the cartons of blood in his refrigerator, then forget this ever happened.

"'Sup, bloodsucker."

The door to the recording booth bounced off the padded wall. Otis strode inside, a shit-eating grin stretched over his cheeks. Two steps into the room, his nostrils flared, and that smile slid right off his face.

The werewolf eyed Zacharias carefully.

"What happened in here?" For once, he sounded serious. His eyebrows pinched as he scanned the room, then twitched up his forehead when his gaze landed on the tiny smear of blood. "Oh, shit."

Zacharias grunted, annoyed. "Indeed. You can hold off on sharpening your stakes; I haven't murdered anyone in your recording booth."

Otis snorted, his expression easy again as he strode to the glass divider. With a lick of his thumb, the tiny smear of Claire's blood was wiped away.

Jealousy curled through Zacharias' gut, but he forced his face to stay blank. It was ridiculous to feel territorial about a smudge of dried blood. Blood from someone he hated, no less.

Pathetic.

"You must have had a hell of a shift," Otis said, apparently reading his mind. He scrubbed at the glass again with his sleeve, eyes flicking to Zacharias through the glass. "You could have called, you know. We'd have cleaned this off hours ago."

Zacharias shrugged. He didn't have a good excuse for not calling for help. Not one that didn't make him sound insane or pathetically blood-struck.

Damn Claire Ramsden.

"Anyway." Otis clapped his hands together, jolting Zacharias out of his brooding. "Drinks? I bet you need a Bloody Mary after that."

One or ten, Zacharias inwardly grumbled, but he gave a casual shrug. He'd already been for drinks with the wolf once recently; if he appeared too eager, Otis might get the wrong impression. He might think they were friends, or some other equally horrendous arrangement.

Zacharias didn't do 'friends'. Not for decades now. It was easier to stay detached, to keep apart, and not constantly lose people.

On the other hand, his fangs had been fully extended for the last six hours. He'd accidentally bitten into his own lip more times than he could count, and if he didn't wet his tongue with blood soon, the worst of his instincts would kick in.

"Alright," he said stiffly. "I'll fetch my jacket."

The walk along the hallway to his shared office was interminable. Otis chattered at his shoulder, apparently unconcerned that Zacharias barely grunted in response. He talked about the station; about plans for new programs and features; about repairs in this hovel of a building. And he volunteered it all unprompted, just giving parts of himself up with no suspicion or expectation of return.

Zacharias cleared his throat as they rounded a corner. He could do this.

"That sounds good," he muttered, as Otis paused for breath in his plans for renovations. Something about new wiring. Otis shot him a grin, then launched straight back in.

Gods. Well, Zacharias had done his part. He tuned the werewolf out for the last stretch of hallway.

It was obvious that something was wrong when they were still meters away. The door was ajar, open three inches, and Angie, the cupid Zacharias shared his office with, was fastidious about locking up behind her. The lights were off inside, but the band poster on the door was knocked askew.

Zacharias drew a deep breath through his nose.

Someone had been here.

Beside him, Otis' monologue stuttered to a stop. The wolf sucked in a breath too, his eyes narrowing as they picked up their stride.

He wouldn't take kindly to an invader in his station. The wolves were all about territory.

The door swung open under Zacharias' palm, creaking on its hinges. Even with the lights off, the destruction was plain to see: papers were shredded and torn and tossed on the floor, coating the carpet. A filing cabinet had been knocked on its side, its drawers lolling open. The potted plant from the cupid's shelf had been tossed on her desk, the pot cracked and the soil scattered over the wood. And Zacharias' belongings—his work computer, his jacket, his damn gym bag—were piled on his desk and drenched in pink paint.

A pair of paint-splattered overalls flashed across his mind.

Claire Ramsden. It had to be her. She'd stomped in here bristling for a fight, and when he'd put her in her place, she'd

retaliated. A low growl was building in the back of Otis'
throat, his huge hands curled into fists as he stared around
the destruction.

"There will be consequences." He spoke quietly: a deadly
promise. It wasn't about Zacharias, not really. It was about his
station. His turf.

Zacharias pinched the bridge of his nose and thought of
Claire Ramsden's freckles.

What the hell had she done?

* * *

It was distressingly easy to track Claire Ramsden. Even
with a grumpy, growling werewolf at his shoulder, Zacharias
barely took a single wrong turn as he followed her scent
down the sidewalk. They trailed her across town, led only
by the humming need in Zacharias' blood and the wisps of her
delicious scent on the breeze.

Zacharias didn't mention the burning in his gut. The way he
needed to set eyes on her again like he'd once needed air. He'd
rather not think about it, and besides—they weren't looking
for her for that.

Otis wanted a word, that was all. About the insult to his
station. And for some damnable reason, Zacharias felt the
need to referee. To ensure the werewolf didn't get carried
away in scaring the fragile human.

Otis was so worked up, every word he spoke came out in a
snarl. He didn't even trust himself to track, allowing Zacharias'
less sensitive nose to lead the way so his hunting instincts were
kept at bay.

It didn't matter. Zacharias wanted to howl it at the sky. It was invasive, yes, a violation of his property. More than anything, he regretted the damage to Angie's plant. But it was a foolish move on Claire Ramsden's part, and—if anyone bothered to ask his opinion—one they'd do better to ignore.

Supernaturals would never be trusted above humans, not even in Boiling River. All anyone else would see was a vampire and a werewolf threatening a defenseless human woman. Never mind that she'd thrown the first punch; that she'd started this ridiculous crusade over nothing.

No. Better to take the hit, improve station security and move on. It was a hard lesson, but one Zacharias had learned several times over his long years.

"Are you sure you want to do this?" he ground out as they marched down the street. Otis huffed, his breath fogging in front of his face, and didn't deign to reply.

It was a quirk of the desert. The days were baking hot, the sun roasting the town alive, but the temperatures plummeted in the night until the residents' breath crystallized in the air. Some mornings, the rocks strewn about the landscape glittered with frost before the sun rose.

"It won't look good," Zacharias said quietly. "For us. For the station. They'll see it as a harmless prank."

Otis' head jerked, his jaw clenched tight, but he kept walking.

Fine. This was clearly happening. Zacharias would deal with this shit show, make sure the idiot woman was safe, then suck down the nearest carton of blood he could find. The last thing they needed was two supernaturals on the verge of losing control.

Claire Ramsden's trail entered the now closed Silver Bullet, where it lingered and strengthened. She'd been here for several hours, no doubt toasting her daring prank with the other humans. Then it spilled back out onto the street, joined by another human female, and they'd weaved down the sidewalk together.

They'd headed away from her bungalow, Zacharias noted, only slightly ashamed that he knew that. Which meant they'd stayed up when the Silver Bullet closed, and set off into Boiling River to wreak more havoc.

It was a small town. Bustling and busy, certainly, and constantly filled with tourists. But there was only one place that people went after the Silver Bullet closed. Hex Mex was rougher, seedier, with pulsing music and drinks flowing until dawn. It was a favorite with the town's supernaturals, who often preferred the night, and with humans who wanted to mix with danger.

That sounded like Claire Ramsden, Zacharias thought grimly. The pretty, foolish woman had truly poked the hornet's nest.

Chapter Seven

*H*ex Mex was a complete dive, but it was Boiling River's dive. A town institution. The high school students grew up trying to buy fake IDs so they could sneak in early. The tourists came in droves, waving dog-eared travel guides and ordering from the overpriced themed cocktails.

The Fang-Rattler. A Howling Orgasm. That sort of thing.

Claire had spent plenty of late nights here over the years, though she always told herself the next morning it'd be the last. The fact was, after Silver Bullet closed at midnight, there weren't many places to go in town if you were restless. Wide awake. Or driven half out of your mind by a glamor-happy vampire.

Claire was restless, alright. Even now, safely away from that husky voice on the radio, her skin tingled and her blood rushed through her veins. She tossed back a shot of tequila, coughing at the burn in her throat, then sucked hard at her wedge of lime. Bree whooped next to her at the bar, her hips swinging to the beat, the neon Hex Mex stamp glowing on her bare wrist.

"Yes, girl!" Bree hollered over the steady thump of music. "I'm so sick of being the only one awake past 1am!"

Working in Silver Bullet, Bree was practically nocturnal. She got bored being the only human awake. Claire wiped her mouth on the back of her hand and scanned the crowd.

"Can you see anyone?"

They'd come here for one purpose: to scratch Claire's vamp-induced itch. Bree had accepted the mission with outright glee, insisting on 'fixing' Claire's makeup before they left Silver Bullet. She'd drawn swooping cat-eye liner and a dusky pink lips onto Claire's unimpressed face.

It was a hookup, Claire reasoned. Not a date. Surely the fine details of her look didn't matter. And besides, no amount of lipstick could smarten up her painter's overalls.

Now that they were here, though, she was glad of the extra armor. Hex Mex was crawling with supernaturals, and that meant a sea of uncannily beautiful faces. She recognised the radio station's cupid, sat with her legs crossed on a stool, her glossy black hair curling under her chin. The woman smirked as she eyed the dance floor, tapping her teeth with her straw. Then she glanced around for witnesses, before blowing a kiss towards a nearby dancing couple.

The effect was immediate. The couple lunged for each other, legs slotting together as their mouths crashed into a kiss. The cupid preened, leaning back against the bar, then caught Claire's stare.

Her almond eyes widened. She glanced around guiltily, then shrugged and gave a wink.

Claire looked away, annoyed. She was seriously tired of these supernaturals toying with the human locals.

"Loads of people," Bree said, answering a question Claire had already forgotten asking. "Humans and supes. Take your pick, Claire-Bear."

Bree had been thrilled to overhear Mabel's nickname for Claire on a visit to the bungalow. She'd cackled so hard, she nearly tripped and fell in the rockery.

"I don't..." Claire stared into the crowd. "I don't know."

This was her idea, damn it, but now that they were here, something felt... off. Her instincts screamed at her to call this off, to go back to the bungalow and deal with this itch herself. There was nothing wrong with the crowd here; no one was fighting, or sloppy drunk, and the club's troll bouncers were strict with creeps. But everywhere she looked, she thought she saw long, curling brown hair and crimson eyes.

Claire blinked hard. It wasn't him. It was a tourist in one of those alien shirts, and he looked nothing like the radio vamp.

She blew out a breath. "It's not going to happen. Let's get out of here."

Beside her, Bree squawked in protest, her drink tipped to her mouth. But it was the movement over her shoulder that froze Claire in her tracks.

It was him. The asshole vamp. And one seriously pissed off werewolf. The guy at his side bristled with anger, his chest heaving with every breath, and his lip curled up in a snarl.

Claire swallowed.

"Um. Can we help you?"

Surely her little visit wasn't that big of a deal. They didn't even lock the radio station doors, and all she'd done was return the vamp's stupid freaking note. The blood smear was childish, she'd admit, but it was hardly worth tracking her down in Hex Mex. Hell, the vampire had barely been flustered. He was in complete control. Annoyingly so.

The vamp said nothing, his watchful eyes flicking between her and the werewolf. Claire raised her eyebrows and crossed her arms, trying not to wince when Bree staggered around to face them and stepped on her foot.

"You..." Bree jabbed a finger at the werewolf. "I know you. Whisky sour. You're a pain in my ass."

The werewolf didn't even glance down. He snarled at Claire over her friend's head, the noise cutting through the blare of music.

A scarred hand rested on the werewolf's shoulder and squeezed lightly. The snarl subsided, but the guy kept his glare fixed on Claire.

"Otis here came to issue a warning." Hearing the vampire's voice again sent a jolt down Claire's spine. She jerked her gaze to his, her pulse hammering, and squeezed her damp hands into fists behind her back. "He doesn't take kindly to trespassers. Nor to destruction of station property."

Even though she was jittery with fear, Claire managed to roll her eyes.

"Oh, please. A squirt of cleaning spray and it'll be gone."

The vampire's jaw tightened at the reminder. "Not the blood. The mess in my office."

Relief and irritation ballooned in Claire's chest, side by side. She didn't know what the hell these two idiots were snarling about, but it had nothing to do with her. Her shoulders dropped an inch, and she reached out to drag Bree away from the werewolf by the back of her black shirt.

"You're mistaken. I've done nothing to your office, vamp, and if you idiots don't leave me the hell alone, I'll report you both for stalking."

The vampire's eyes flashed, and for the first time the werewolf's brow smoothed. His snarl dropped away, and it was like a curtain closing: one moment he was a bloodthirsty predator, the next, a confused, friendly guy.

"It wasn't you?" He turned to the vampire. "I thought you said you could smell her?"

The vampire had the grace to look embarrassed. His eyes flicked to Claire again, unsure now, then he dismissed her with a jerk of his chin.

"Her blood messed me up. Let's go. We might still get something from the office."

"You're welcome!" Claire yelled at their retreating backs. "Maybe invest in some cameras, assholes!"

Bree swayed next to her, her frown fuzzy as she stared after the werewolf. Claire snatched their jackets and bundled her to the exit, ignoring her friend's mumbles about whisky sours.

This was a bust. She'd come here to take the edge off the jitters the vamp gave her—the way her skin felt three sizes too small. But now that she'd seen him again in person, felt the scorching heat of his eyes on her skin, she was gone again. Out of her damn mind with need.

None of these other guys would cut it. Not after seeing those crimson eyes again.

She'd drop Bree home. Make a beeline to her bungalow. And put the contents of her bedside drawer to good use.

* * *

The horizon was tinged pink by the time Claire finally got home. The stars blinked from the inky darkness overhead, and the sky paled and blushed as it stretched towards the mountains. Claire yawned so hard her jaw cracked, shutting the cab door and waving at the driver through the window.

What a night. What a gods-damned night.

The soft dirt crunched under her sneakers as she walked up her front path. Her bungalow looked weird at night with no lights on and no crashes echoing from the kitchen. When Dad was still here, he was constantly forgetting to switch off the lights, and crashing pots around as he made a midnight snack.

It had driven her mad, but she missed it now. Sometimes she left a lamp on just to feel like he was near.

The back of her neck tickled as she reached the garden gate, sliding the bolt across and nudging it open. She never used to bother closing it, but since she found that note in her kitchen…

Maybe she should get an alarm, too.

Her rock garden was tinged silver in the moonlight. She brushed her fingertips over cactus spines as she passed, so pathetically grateful that at least some of her dad's plants had survived her care. A throat cleared by her kitchen door and Claire jolted, whacking her hand into the cactus.

"Ow." She stuffed the edge of her hand in her mouth, sucking at the brand new cuts and glaring at the shadow by her doorway. She didn't have to call him into the moonlight. She knew exactly who it was.

It felt inevitable, somehow, that he'd be here. That realization slid uneasily through her gut.

"Wha' 'o you wan'?" she mumbled around her palm. The vampire sucked in a sharp breath from her doorway.

He was smelling her. Scenting the blood on her hand. Claire's pulse thrummed in her neck.

"You broke into the station," he said quietly. This was not a man who ever had to raise his voice. He spoke, and even the crickets hushed up to listen.

Claire eyed the distance to the kitchen door. Weighed her chances of darting inside and slamming the door in his face.

Slim to none, she decided. And that was without his vamp reflexes.

"I already told you." She licked her lips, and the shadow twitched. "I didn't mess up your office."

A light was on in Mabel's window. Perhaps if she yelled out—screamed loud enough—the banshee would come to check on her.

"Your neighbor is asleep," the shadow said flatly. "I heard her snoring from halfway down the street."

"She'll wake up if I scream."

"I'm not here to hurt you." He sounded almost offended. Claire raised her chin and stared into the deepest shadows, eyes searching for the flash of crimson.

"Then why are you here?"

The vampire sighed. His boots scraped over the dirt as he pushed off the wall. When he stepped into the moonlight, the sight of him was a punch to the chest. Dark jeans clinging to muscled thighs; a black sweater stretched over a toned chest. And that hair, curling in escaped strands around his sharp jaw.

Claire's breath sawed into her lungs with a wheeze.

"I want you to stop." His voice was harsh. A muscle ticked in his jaw. "I want you to stay away."

Claire snorted. "You're at *my* house, vamp. You're the one who keeps following me home." It should bother her more, but the only instincts that were screaming at her were not fight or flight. No; they were another 'f' word. Claire licked again at her pricked hand, scowling at the stone path.

He'd seen her mosaics. It wasn't fair. Those tiles were personal, handmade, and he'd broken in here and stolen a glimpse at this piece of her.

"Let's make a deal. I'll never set foot in the radio station again, and you'll stay the hell off my property. You won't hunt me down in bars, or accuse me of whatever crimes you feel like. You'll back the hell off."

His jaw flexed, and she could practically hear his fangs grind. But the vampire gave a short, sharp nod and stepped forward. "Deal."

Not thinking straight, Claire thrust out her hand to shake. His nostrils flared, and he leaned away from her hand like it was a spitting cobra.

"I rather think not."

Claire dropped her bleeding hand way too late. "Sorry. I didn't think."

"A common occurrence, I'm sure," the vampire sneered, and moved to edge around her on the path. She rolled her eyes and stomped straight to the door.

"One more thing." She spun around before she put her key in the lock. She had to get this out. And the vampire crossed his arms and waited, his crimson eyes lit up by the paling sky. "I know you're using your glamor on the radio. Somehow. I know it. And I want you to know it won't work. I'd rather die than ever touch a vamp."

It was never real lust or love with a vampire. She knew that from her front-row seat to her mother's downfall. It was just chemicals and magic and then heartbreak all the way.

She'd never give into it. No matter how much her body screamed for this man.

His lip curled at her words, his eyes flicking down her body with clear disdain.

"Don't flatter yourself. A woman like you would not be worth the magic."

It stung—gods, she hated that it stung, but she jerked her head and turned back to the door. It was over. They'd had it out, and this was the last she'd see of him. She'd never listen to that stupid radio show again, and she'd start carrying ear buds for when it played in public. Her key slid into the lock, the keyhole easy to find in the dawning light.

A hiss sounded behind her, and Claire wheeled around, the door banging open behind her. The vampire stared at the sunrise bruising the horizon, horror etched on his face. He whipped around, searching for a patch of shadow. Somewhere to hide and wait out the day.

Nothing. That was the problem with desert valleys. The sun found you wherever you hid.

His eyes darted to her, conflict warring behind them—like he was too proud, even now, to ask for help.

"Oh, come *on*." Claire marched down the stone path and grabbed his sweater in her fist. She yanked him back to the door and shoved him inside just as the sun broke over the mountains.

The vampire hissed and dropped to his knees, sheltering beneath the cabinets. His eyes darted from her, to the door, to the shaft of sunshine spilling through the window, then back to Claire. Anger and discomfort distorted his handsome face, like he was pissed off at *her* for saving his useless afterlife.

Claire shut the back door. Crossed to the cabinets and fetched a glass of water. She offered it mutely to the vampire on her kitchen floor, who shook his head with a jerk.

Perfect. Wonderful. Her stalker was in her kitchen. And not only that, he was stuck in her bungalow until night fell again.

The contents of her bedside cabinet called to her down the

hall. Claire cursed under her breath and squeezed her thighs together.

She'd never get any freaking relief. And now he was here—her own brand of torture, glowering at her like this was *her* idea.

Gods. What a night.

Chapter Eight

Zacharias slid lower to the kitchen tiles and cursed whichever gods were tormenting him for fun. A shaft of buttery morning sunlight shone through the window overhead, dust motes spinning lazily in the glow. He was safe below the window—he wouldn't burn to ash, at least—but his pride had never taken such a blow.

"How old are you, vampire?"

Claire Ramsden leaned against her sink, arms crossed and her foot tapping. She looked pale and drawn this morning, the blue-tinged shadows under her eyes more stark in the warm sunshine. She still wore those filthy overalls, and her red hair was rumpled. The faint scent of alcohol drifted from her, eking from her pores, but even that could not suppress her scent.

Tangerines. Basil. Turpentine. And rich, coppery blood. Her pulse point thudded in her throat, drawing his starving eyes, and Zacharias' fangs lengthened in his mouth.

"Two hundred and seventeen," he muttered, keeping his lips close to hide his fangs. She tilted her head and smirked scornfully down at him from the safety of the sunshine.

"Oh? And how long since you were turned?"

Zacharias frowned, trying to force his muddled thoughts back so far. He didn't like to think of *before*, of his time back in England. Of living twelve-to-a-room with his sprawling family; of the dark, damp mines.

"One hundred and eighty four years." Roughly. Give or take. Claire nodded and pushed off the sink to stand upright, her eyes hard as she stared down at him. Her fingers flexed where she gripped her forearms, tight enough to drain her fingertips of blood.

Zacharias' gut clenched. He'd suffered through an entire torturous shift with her blood on the divider, then hours playing cat and mouse with Otis. Zacharias thought longingly of the Bloody Mary he was promised—hell, even one of those stale cartons of blood in the radio station vending machines.

He was so gods-damned hungry.

"And in those one hundred and eighty four years, did you not learn to stay out of the sun?" She was enunciating each word, prissy like a school teacher, and Zacharias stiffened where his back rested against the cabinets. She dared to lecture him, this human exercise in poor judgement? His jaw clenched, and his left fang punctured his lower lip.

"In your time in this town, did you not learn never to taunt a vampire with your blood?"

She huffed, eyes rolling, and Zacharias suppressed a smirk. Claire Ramsden was enjoyable to rile up. And she was riled, no matter how much she might hate him. He could scent her arousal on the air; could see from her bright eyes and the flush creeping up her neck. As if she could sense the sudden pique of his interest, she stormed out of the kitchen without another word.

Zacharias leaned back against the cabinets. He stared up at the ceiling, cursing any and all gods within a ten mile radius. Then he slid his phone out of his pocket and hit dial.

Otis' phone rang thirty times before going to voicemail. He tried the radio station next, but these were the dead hours when only a few people were in the building, and they were tucked away in the booths.

A car, maybe. If he could get hold of a car with tinted windows, and covered every inch of his skin between the door and the vehicle...

Of course, the tiniest slip and he'd be a pile of ashes. Another handful of dirt in the desert. No; Zacharias hadn't survived nearly two hundred years as a vampire by taking unnecessary risks, no matter what Claire Ramsden thought.

Apart from this morning. He couldn't account for it. He'd never in all his afterlife been so distracted as to forget the gods-damned dawn. Zacharias dug the heels of his palms into his eyes, groaning at his own stupidity.

"You can come through, you know."

Her voice called from deeper in the house. Zacharias briefly toyed with the idea of refusing, before dismissing it as even more humiliating than his current situation. He could not sulk on these kitchen tiles for the entire day. He could not have her stepping over his legs and pulling out drawers over his head to cook.

Really, he thought as he slid towards the doorway, careful to keep below the shaft of daylight, he should have broken in and looked around her bungalow when he had the chance. At least then he'd know where the windows were, and there would be no risk of rounding a corner and bursting into flames—

"There you are." Claire Ramsden stood over him, offering a hand. Her non-bloodied hand. Zacharias eyed it but did not move, and she let out a huff. "I've closed all the curtains. You'll be safer through here."

It could be a trap, of course—she clearly loathed him, and there would be no evidence if she vacuumed up his ashes—but the constant onslaught of her scent was wearing down his defences. He was muddled. Frayed. So viciously hungry; so horrendously turned on. Zacharias grunted and gripped her hand, pushing to his feet in the shadowed doorway.

She really had closed the curtains, he noted, glancing over her shoulder. The living room was dim, the dark shapes of lumpy sofas scattered over the floorboards. His eyes adjusted quickly, picking out the faded lilac and green pattern of the rug spread over the floor.

"Keep away from me, vamp." She dropped his hand like it stung. "And get out of my house the second dusk falls."

"Zacharias," is all he said, voice hoarse. She frowned at him and he glared back. "My name is Zacharias. Not *vamp*."

She'd saved his afterlife; it shouldn't matter, not really, but it bothered him more than he liked to admit that he knew her name and she didn't care to know his. A name was important. Humanizing. And he'd been a human man, once.

A human man who'd have looked at a woman like Claire Ramsden and fallen to his knees. Too bad she was tiresome harpy if you happened to be undead.

Claire paused, then nodded quickly and left, her sneakers squeaking on the floorboards. She took most of her scent with her, but it still lingered in every room, on every surface.

Zacharias sucked in a breath through his mouth and winced at the thirst burning his throat. His fangs prodded insistently into his lip, and he'd been uncomfortably swollen in his jeans for hours, now.

It was going to be a long day.

* * *

Forty minutes later, he knocked on Claire Ramsden's bedroom door. They had been the most torturous minutes of his life, as he listened with heightened senses as Claire shut herself away in her bedroom and set about easing the unbearable tension between them. He'd heard every sigh and whimper as though he'd had his ear pressed to the door—never mind that he'd clapped a pillow to each side of his head. His cock had strained against his jeans, demanding he take the same relief, but he scowled at the living room bookcase, resolute.

He would not touch himself like a secretive teenager in the house of a woman who hated him. He had some pride, damn it.

She'd finished with a muffled cry—as though she too were making use of a pillow—then gone directly to her adjoining bathroom and cranked the shower to life. And so Zacharias had waited, thirst searing his throat, as Claire Ramsden washed away last night's drinks and sweat and desire, then wrapped herself in a fluffy towel.

He gave her time to dress, his knuckles white as he gripped his phone. Then he rapped on her bedroom door, wincing as it rattled on its hinges.

"Can I help you with something?" She threw his own words from the station back in his face, her expression plainly saying that she would rather stick a fork in her eye. Claire Ramsden crossed her arms, her damp hair speckling her pale green t-shirt. She wore a fresh set of overalls, though these were paint-splattered too.

"I need the WiFi password."

She let out a shocked laugh. "And I need a million dollars."

Zacharias closed his eyes for a long moment, sucking in a breath. *Patience.* He needed to exercise patience, else this foolish woman would regret letting her into his home.

"I need blood," he ground out. "Now. Right now. I can order some online." His eyes dropped to her pulse leaping in her throat, hoping she'd take the hint. If he got hungry enough, it wouldn't matter that she'd saved him. That he'd rather gnaw off his own leg than bite the unwilling. The predator inside him would take control, and they'd both be lost in the fallout.

"Hm." She chewed on her bottom lip, eyeing him like she didn't believe him. Her bare toes scrunched on the floorboards, and she tilted her head before letting out a huff. "Fine." She threw up her hands. "If it'll get you off my back."

She held out a palm and he stared at it. She raised her eyebrows.

A smirk tugged her lips when he slapped his phone into her waiting palm. She tapped the screen, entering the password and watching it connect before handing it back.

"Thank you."

"Don't download anything weird," was all she said.

He wanted to ask what on earth she thought he'd download, but pain seared through his throat, dragging him back on task. Zacharias opened the Screams on Wheels app and ordered enough blood to glut a pride of lions. He waited, nerves prickling, until the little tick glowed on his screen, confirming his order. Expected wait: thirty minutes.

Relief flooded through him, even as the thirst tore through

his throat. He shot Claire a faint smile, nodded, then turned and walked back down the hall. Time to put as much distance as he could between himself and this ripe, blushing human.

Chapter Nine

*C*laire had never received a delivery of blood before. She didn't know what she'd expected—little glass bottles in a crate, perhaps—but she was greeted with a keg. The delivery gnome heaved it out of his van, the weight thudding into the dirt of her front yard. His narrowed eyes flicked between the heavy keg and the distant doorway, then he grinned at her, flashing a gold tooth.

"Good luck, miss."

Claire opened her mouth to argue, but the gnome slammed the van doors shut and vaulted back into the driver's seat. He peeled away with a screech of tires, the van tipping onto two wheels as he rounded a corner at full speed. The whine of his engine faded away as Claire looked at the giant keg of blood, propped her hands on her hips, and swore.

That gods-damned vampire. *Zacharias.* What an ass.

It took an embarrassingly long amount of time for her to drag the keg to her front door. She couldn't lift it—there was no way, not with her freaking noodle arms—so she gritted her teeth and yanked it along the ground, the curved rim digging a shallow trench through her dirt path. After ten minutes, Zacharias opened the front door and watched her, face tense.

"Judge all you want, vamp," she huffed, straining to pull it another few inches. In the corner of her eye, she saw him twitch with irritation. The name thing really bothered him. "Maybe next time you should order a couple of bottles instead of a whole damn keg."

He muttered something from the doorway, but she didn't catch it. She was too busy panting and grunting, her palms slick with sweat as she dragged the keg up her path. When she reached the lip of the front door, she let the keg drop, dancing her toes out of the way just in time.

Zacharias looked helplessly at the keg, out in the sunshine, then back at Claire. She scrubbed at her face.

"Oh, for gods' sake."

Claire squatted behind the keg, placing her palms against the warm metal. The desert sun was quick to heat every surface; she could feel it tickling the skin at the back of her neck. At least a breeze wafted over her too, stirring the sweaty strands of her hair.

"Ready?" Claire asked, licking her lips and glancing up at the vampire. He nodded, holding up his palms as though they were about to play catch. Claire shook her head, biting back the tirade of curse words on her tongue, and shoved with all her might. She slammed into the keg with her full body weight, grunting as it teetered forwards an inch.

"Gods...damn...it!" Claire screamed, her sneakers digging into the dirt. She pushed harder, and finally, *finally,* the top of the keg tilted into the shade of the doorway. The vampire snatched the rim and lifted it inside, as though it were nothing more than a heavy backpack. And Claire toppled with it, slamming to her knees in the desert dirt.

The vampire—Zacharias—jerked forward, reaching for her, then snatched his hands back when he remembered the sun. Claire scowled up at him, her chest heaving and her kneecaps buzzing with pain.

"Worst. House guest. Ever."

He winced, but turned to the keg, screwing it open. "Thank you," he threw over his shoulder as Claire stomped past, trailing dusty footprints over her own living room rug.

"My freaking pleasure," Claire growled, wiping her hands on her overalls as she marched to her studio. She needed paints. Charcoals and the sweet smell of paper. She needed to lose herself in her work.

More than anything, she needed to forget the husky vampire gorging on blood in her living room.

* * *

Claire had always loved to draw. It was her *thing*: in high school, when her friends had football or math or theater, she had art. She was the arty one. She'd even had a tiny business for a while, selling custom drawings to her classmates for a fee.

Dad roared with laughter when she'd finally admitted that, filled with guilt one evening in the kitchen. He'd ruffled her hair and asked to see some of these drawings. Then he'd bought one—a pen and ink drawing of the statue in the Boiling River town square, the one that moved in the night—and stuck it on the refrigerator.

It was still there, crammed between take-out menus and last year's calendar and postcards from when Bree went backpacking for six months. She should really take that down, Claire mused. She could bring it to Dad in the nursing home.

If art was her happy place, this vampire had kicked down the door. She couldn't freaking concentrate, couldn't get in the flow, not with him so near. His watchful eyes, the knowing curl of his mouth, the way he observed and hardly ever spoke. And when he did talk, *that voice.*

Claire sucked in a shuddering breath. Just a few more hours. Then she'd never have to see him again.

Usually, when she was wired like this, she blew off her work projects and her paid commissions and played around until her nerves settled. There was no point spoiling good work she'd already done, and sometimes when she was keyed up, she did her best work. The work that won her a place in galleries, or that sold at auction.

It was rare, but it paid her bills for months when that happened.

This time, though, her hand trembled too hard. She couldn't get a proper grip on her paintbrushes or pens, and she didn't trust herself to measure out powders or mix paints. Claire stuck to charcoals, the black lumps melting in her sweaty grip, and drew wrong line after wrong line.

"Damn it!" She tossed the charcoal onto her work table and glared at the sketchbook propped on her easel. She'd moved it to the window, hoping to draw the mountains if nothing else. Boiling River knew how to show off a view. But her lines were wobbly, first too shy, then too harsh, and her last hour's work looked like an amateur's first attempt.

"Damn it," she muttered again, and rubbed a palm over her tired eyes. Too late, she remembered the charcoal on her hands, no doubt streaking her face with gray.

"Trouble?" A low voice rasped from the doorway. Claire tossed a glare at the vampire over her shoulder. He looked better already, his red eyes bright and his skin glowing with health. Even his dark hair seemed glossier where it curled in strands around his face.

"I can't..." Claire tore the page from her sketchbook and scrunched it up, launching it into the corner with a dozen other paper balls. "I can't think straight."

"Because of me," the vampire said, matter of fact. Like it was a given; like women regularly lost their minds in his presence, blood rushing from their brains to the spot between their legs. Claire ground her teeth, irritation flaring in her chest.

"Because I don't want you here," she corrected him. The vampire hummed—not like he didn't believe her, but like he felt the same way—and strolled inside her studio, hands in his pockets. The late afternoon sun had tracked away from the window, and he could move around the room without fear of burning to a crisp. He wandered slowly around the walls, inspecting everything from her stack of finished works to her half-way done projects and the shelves of her supplies. When he reached the wash station in the corner, he picked up a jar of turpentine and sniffed it, humming again.

Claire shook her head and turned back to her view of the mountains. Freaking vampires.

"You're an artist."

Claire adjusted the grip on her charcoal and privately rolled her eyes.

"That's very observant of you, vampire."

"Zacharias."

"That's very observant of you, Zacharias." She'd meant it to sound mocking, but instead his name sounded weirdly intimate. Claire cleared her throat, ignoring the prickle of tiny hairs standing up on her arms.

Her hand drifted across the paper, following the arc and fall of the mountain line. The jagged peaks; the towering columns of stone; then the smooth dips and ledges. Gradually, the sound of her breath faded away, along with the creak of the floorboards under the vampire's boots.

The charcoal danced across the page, shading and sketching, and Claire stared so hard her eyes went dry. When she finally remembered to blink, resting her arm for a moment, the bare lines of the landscape were drawn.

"Not bad," she muttered to herself, more relieved than pleased.

"Impressive," the vampire agreed, stood directly behind her. He watched over her shoulder, his hands thrust deep in his pockets and a rueful twist to his mouth. His gaze flicked to hers. "I never could draw. Not even after two hundred years' practice."

"Anyone can learn," Claire heard herself saying, even as she preened under his praise. "There are loads of good tutorials online these days."

Zacharias tilted his head, eyes back on her sketchbook. "To a certain level, perhaps. But you didn't learn to draw like that from videos online."

It was true. No one could teach you to lose yourself in the page; you had to learn that part on your own. It pleased her, for some ridiculous reason, to hear him acknowledge that. To imply she had talent. Bree and Olivia were supportive, of course, but when they came to her studio, they didn't really *look*.

Claire swallowed around the sudden lump in her throat and

turned back to her sketchbook. She shifted the charcoal in her grip.

"You can try for yourself, if you like. There are spare sketchbooks and supplies."

"I'd rather watch," he said, low and honeyed, and shivers skittered down her spine.

"Alright." Claire licked her lips. "But don't put me off. And don't bite me," she added as an afterthought, suddenly aware of her throat, bared by her hair piled up in a bun, and the vampire's mouth oh so close.

"I couldn't drink another drop," he promised, amusement curling through his voice, and Claire stifled a smile as she glanced back out the window.

It was harmless. A few hours of entertainment for him, and she seemed to focus better knowing exactly where he was. A mutually beneficial arrangement.

Claire took a deep breath and reached for the sketchbook.

Chapter Ten

*C*laire Ramsden worked like a dog. A charcoal-smeared, paint-stained dog. When she finally emerged from her studio, her eyes were bright and wild strands of red hair escaped the messy bun atop her head.

Zacharias watched her out of the corner of his eye. He'd settled into the living room again after an hour of watching her work. Truthfully, he could have stayed there all day, but her scent was intoxicating and her throat maddeningly close. The warmth of her body washed over his front as he stood behind her, and several times he had to close his eyes and breathe through his mouth.

No. He wouldn't stand around panting like an animal, no matter how fascinating her work. So he'd retreated to the safety of the living room and taken desperate gulps of blood from the keg.

It was cold. Tangy from the metal container. The equivalent, he imagined, of a soggy gas station egg sandwich.

But it was blood. It kept the thirst from tearing his throat to pieces, and it kept Claire Ramsden safe from his worst instincts. It was the least he could do, really, considering the way she'd saved him—not just from the sun, but by heaving his keg up the front path. He'd bitten his tongue watching her, swallowing back the helpful hints he somehow knew she would not appreciate. And now, as he sprawled catlike over her sofa, flicking through a book of photography, her sweet little grunts played on a loop in his head.

"Can you even see those in the dark?" Claire leaned over the back of his sofa, her scent wafting over him. Zacharias sat up, surreptitiously adjusting himself in his jeans.

"As well as in full daylight. Better, even." His voice was rough from the morning's thirst, and from not speaking for hours. He spent plenty of days without speaking to another soul in his underground apartment, but he'd gotten into an unfortunate habit of muttering to himself just to hear someone speak.

He couldn't do that here. She already thought the worst of him.

Claire looked over, her gaze boring into his eyes, scanning his crimson irises with naked curiosity. It was a step up from revulsion, at least. He blinked and looked away.

"The shadows are getting long." Claire crossed the rug, poking her head around the side of the curtain. Zacharias took the opportunity to stare shamelessly at her form: a slender waist. Wide, flaring hips, and narrow shoulders. "I expect you'll be able to go soon."

He tried not to let that sting.

"Thank you for today."

She must be exhausted. She hadn't slept since the gods knew when, having dragged him inside her kitchen at dawn then worked the whole day. He suspected she didn't trust him enough to be that vulnerable. To sleep when he was near.

Claire Ramsden didn't feel safe with him. Zacharias scowled at the wall.

"It's okay." To his shock, she let the curtain drop and walked past the spare armchairs to sit next to him. When she plopped down on the sofa cushions, another waft of her scent hit him like a punch to the gut, and she hitched a knee up so she could turn and stare right at him.

"Careful," he gritted out, and he could taste her sudden flash of fear. He wasn't threatening her, didn't want her afraid, but for someone who'd called him 'vamp' since meeting him, she seemed to forget his nature. She played it off, raising her chin and lifting one shoulder.

"Why? Are you going to attack me in my own home?"

A shower of holy water could not have kept Zacharias from rolling his eyes. He slumped back against the opposite arm of the sofa and reached up to tug on a stray lock of his hair.

"I could, I suppose. Do you have anything worth stealing?"

Her snort was gratifying. "Nope."

"Then I suppose you're safe, Claire Ramsden."

He liked saying her full name. It sounded rough in his mouth; it was a name he could get his teeth into. And judging from the blush that tinged her cheeks, she liked it too.

This was a terrible idea. Truly awful. She'd accused him of glamoring her again. But she'd also saved him twice now, and sat beside him on the sofa...

Zacharias reached out before he could overthink it. His fingertips drifted over her cheek, curving round her jaw all the way to her chin, his touch whisper-soft. And Claire Ramsden sucked in a shaky breath, closed her eyes, and let him touch her.

It wasn't fear he tasted on the air now. It was pulsing, thudding arousal. She was drenched with it, burning hot, and as his thumb slid down to stroke at her throat, he heard her heart beat harder. It slammed against her fragile rib cage, lunging for him, seeking him—Zacharias snatched his hand back and placed it firmly on his knee, forcing a smile for her dazed face.

"I'll be gone as soon as the sun sets," he promised. "Then you'll never have to see me again."

* * *

Boiling River came alive at night. With such a large supernatural community, it was inevitable, but even the humans seemed to perk up in the evenings. Perhaps it was the baking heat which scorched the earth during the day. It made them sleepy and dull.

The tourists and locals thronging the main street were not sleepy now. They were raucous, yelling to each other across the road, swigging from brown paper bags and howling with laughter. The evening was cool, a breeze ruffling the crowds as the day's stored heat drifted up from the dirt. By morning, Boiling River would be nipped with cold again, and the cycle would start anew.

A booming laugh that could only belong to Otis echoed down the street. Zacharias hitched his keg higher under his arm and slipped into an alleyway, opting for the maze of back streets over yet another social interaction. Claire Ramsden had been surprisingly pleasant company, but he was still worn thin from a full day spent on edge.

His apartment. That was what he needed. His silently,

blissfully empty apartment, with the gentle lap of pool water and the dance of ripples reflected on his ceiling.

Even starting from the outskirts, a determined pair of legs could cross the width of Boiling River in forty minutes. It was not a large town—the valley would not bear too much life—and in the busiest parts of town, the buildings huddled together obligingly. Zacharias' own building was a few streets away from the town square, near the center of the action but tucked safely out of view. It suited him: he could observe the movements around him, the way he always had, yet stay hidden himself.

Once a pickpocket, always a pickpocket.

Those days were long gone—those months in London after he was turned, scraping a living with his quick fingers and sharp fangs—but old habits died hard. And Zacharias York died even harder.

The French bakery next door to his apartment building was closed, the sign flipped in the doorway even as the lights were still on inside. Zacharias nodded to the owner, Mr Dupont; the most genteel troll he'd met in his two hundred something years. The baker nodded back, green-tinged forehead creased as he swept the bakery floor. His tusks curled out of his mouth and cast an odd shadow, and his meaty hands were dusted with flour.

Sometimes Zacharias regretted his limited diet. It was a cruel loss, especially considering his family could never afford the best food even when he was living. By the time he'd made his undead fortune and sent funds back up north, it was too late for him to enjoy the rewards himself.

Shifting the keg in his grip, Zacharias strode to the entrance of his apartment building. It was pale brick rather than adobe, with curling, wrought iron railings lining the balconies on the upper floors. The usual doorman, Giles, was not at his post, and Zacharias glanced around for the ancient old man as he crossed the lobby.

A groan echoed behind the desk. Zacharias froze, sniffing the air and straining for further noise. The coppery tang of blood was on the air, filling his mouth with saliva and tightening his throat.

There was another groan, a thump, and the drag of something over the tiles. Zacharias placed his keg on the marble floor and rushed around the reception desk.

Giles blinked up at him, eyes unfocused, a puddle of glossy blood on the floor. Hunger roared to life in Zacharias' gut, and he smothered his nose and mouth in his sleeve as he dug his phone from his pocket.

Someone would come, he thought wildly, as he dialed 911. Someone else would deal with the old man's injury. There was no way he could—

Giles moaned again, weaker than before, and Zacharias cursed and yanked his sweater over his head. Clad in only a gray t-shirt, his bare arm pressed to his nose, he balled his sweater up and pushed it against the cut on Giles' skull. The operator could barely hear his words through the thirst squeezing his throat, but when sirens sounded in the street outside, Giles slumped into the tiles.

"Come on," Zacharias muttered, pressing his bundle harder against the wound. "Don't waste my favorite sweater."

A choked, gurgling laugh came from the lobby floor, and Zacharias' mouth quirked in a grim smile.

It slid off his face as quickly as it came. This was no accident. No slip or tumble. This was an attack on a fragile human man;

a deliberate act of violence. To rob one of the apartments, most likely, or else purely to hurt the weak.

Zacharias' nose wrinkled in distaste.

Something like this would shock the locals. It would draw unwanted press. And it would stoke suspicions towards the town's supernaturals. Especially supernaturals like him—new to Boiling River, already accused of stalking, and now first on the scene of a vicious attack.

Zacharias sighed, rolled his head on his sore neck, and glanced longingly over his shoulder at his keg. The sirens wailed closer, then boots thudded over the marble floor, voices yelling for Zacharias to get down.

He pressed his cheek against the cool marble, spreading his hands where they could see, watching on a horizontal tilt as EMTs dropped to their knees around his doorman. Giles groaned but answered their questions, his voice thready and muffled, and they bundled him onto a stretcher, ready to take to Boiling River's tiny hospital.

No one knew what to do with Zacharias, and that suited him just fine. He stayed pressed to the marble, obligingly still, until the last EMT prodded him with the toe of his boot.

"The cops will want a word."

Zacharias rolled onto his back and stared at the high ceiling. There was a crack in the paint.

"They always do."

Chapter Eleven

*C*laire pushed a trolley of books down the narrow aisle between library stacks. She moved slowly, chewing on the inside of her cheek as Olivia plucked the returns off the trolley one by one and slid them back on their shelves.

"It's just weird, you know?"

By the library's own rules, Olivia should be shushing her. Though Claire's friend had been quiet since high school, she could muster a fierce librarian's glare. She wore her blond hair braided away from her face, and her tortoiseshell reading glasses made her look extra stern. But the Boiling River library was empty first thing in the morning, and there was no one around for Claire to disturb.

"What's weird?"

Olivia spoke to the book in her hand, flipping it over to inspect the spine. There were dark shadows under her eyes behind her glasses; she looked more exhausted than Claire, even though Claire had barely slept in two days.

Freaking insomnia. It was so unfair. Olivia was the one of

the best people around—eternally sweet, patient, and... well. Haunted.

"The radio vamp. Zacharias. It's weird his voice does that to me without a glamor."

Olivia hummed, non-committal. "Some voices are just nice. Why do you think audio books are so popular?"

"His voice isn't *nice*." Claire shoved the squeaky trolley over a bump in the carpet, her grip vicious on the handlebar. "It's freaking invasive. It's like there's a direct wire between his voice box and my vagina."

Olivia huffed a laugh, sliding a book called *Trolls and Tribulations: A History of Bridges* back onto the shelf.

"If he's not using his glamor, there's nothing magical about it." She slid Claire a smirk. "You're just horny."

'Horny' was a paltry word to describe the way the vampire's voice affected Claire. It was like calling the scorching desert 'a bit warm'.

She'd tried to tune into his show again last night, feeling like the worst kind of pervert. But he'd hadn't come on the air, some demon taking his place, and she'd slammed her laptop shut in a flustered sulk.

Was he alright? Did spending the day in her bungalow hurt him somehow? Claire chewed on her thumbnail, redirecting the trolley just before it smashed into the bookshelves. She'd tossed in her bed all night, unable to calm her racing mind, worried about Zacharias.

It was humiliating. She was turning into her mother.

A throat cleared at the end of the aisle, and Claire glanced up to find one of the town's police officers leaning against the stacks. His tawny hair was wild, his arms crossed, and his brown eyes stared directly at her.

"Morning, ladies," the leopard shifter rasped. He smiled but it didn't reach his eyes. "Could I steal you away for a moment, Miss Ramsden?"

Claire swallowed, palms suddenly clammy on the trolley. She nodded, mind racing as she edged beside the bookshelf and squeezed down the aisle. Olivia tried to catch her eye, but Claire stared at her sneakers, her thoughts in a panicked tangle.

Was this about the station again? Had they filed a complaint at her for walking in? Was that even illegal?

And beneath those thoughts, hurt pinched in her chest. Did Zacharias really hate her so much? *Still?* The way he'd touched her cheek, his fingertips brushing over her skin...

"What's this about, Danny?" she asked, forcing brightness into her voice. He slid her a look like he saw right through her, and he probably did. He'd only been a few years ahead in high school, and he knew Boiling River like he knew his own shadow.

"The vampire." He cut to the chase, leading her away from the stacks and rounding on her by the water cooler. "Zacharias York. At the radio station. Do you know him?"

Claire's pulse thudded in her ears. "Yes," she whispered. Danny already knew that, or else why was he here? It was a test, to see if she'd lie to him.

Gods, she wanted to lie. But his eyes bore into hers, pinning her in place.

"He says he spent from dawn until dusk yesterday in your home. Can you verify that?"

Claire frowned. "Yes..."

Danny's eyebrows lifted, then he wiped his face carefully blank. He hadn't expected that. Well, all the Boiling River locals knew the way Claire's mom had left. They all knew her distrust of vampires. He pulled a notebook out of his shirt pocket and scribbled something.

"He got caught out," Claire blurted, suddenly desperate to explain herself. To make sure no one got the wrong idea. "Zacharias got caught off guard by the sunrise, so he came in for shelter. That's all."

The shifter grunted, an interested gleam in his eye. He tapped his pen against his canine, long and sharp even in his human form.

"Would you vouch for him?"

Claire wiped her palms on her shorts. "What does that mean, exactly?"

"Would you vouch for his character? Would you say he's a responsible citizen?"

"I…" Claire's mouth worked uselessly. "I barely know him. We only just met."

The ghost of his touch prickled on her cheek. Again, that fascinated gleam flickered across Danny's face before he smoothed it away. He tucked his notebook in his shirt pocket and gave a brisk nod.

"Thank you, Miss Ramsden—Claire." He turned to go, and Claire grabbed for his sleeve without thinking.

"I don't know him well, but I do trust Zacharias York," she blurted. "He seems like a good man, Danny."

The officer watched her for a moment before nodding, brisk, then strode out of the library. Olivia appeared at Claire's shoulder, her face pale and afraid.

"What's going on, Claire?"

The lump in her throat strangled her speech. Claire coughed and swallowed hard.

"I don't know," she told her friend, eyes on the empty street where the police officer had just stood. "But something tells me it's nothing good."

* * *

Claire snapped at 9pm and charged out her back door. She'd spent the entire day trying to force herself back to normal—to forget Zacharias York.

She ate breakfast burritos with Olivia and helped tidy up the library stacks. She ran errands in town, then headed home to her studio. And she'd stared at the charcoal landscape on her sketchpad, her mind blocked and her hands useless.

Claire couldn't think. Her mind was fuzzy; her thoughts jumbled. She boiled water, then forgot to make coffee. She left her back door wide open without realizing; she moved things around her home, then forgot where she'd put them. She even lost her favorite pair of overalls somehow, never mind that she specifically remembered hanging them on the line in her backyard.

She was a mess. A frazzled mess, and her body surged between clumsy numbness and jangling nerves all day.

It was almost a relief when the sun set. Claire had given up any hope of getting work done hours ago; today was officially about getting through it. If she had a lick of sense, she'd go and see Bree at the Silver Bullet, or she'd bundle up in blankets on her sofa, eat ice cream from the tub, and watch crappy movies.

She had no sense. Not even a lick. And now she was out beneath the stars, heart hammering in her chest.

Claire's boots crunched in the dirt as she strode toward town. She was not headed for the Silver Bullet. And damn her, she'd showered, drawn on eyeliner, and changed out of her work overalls into jeans and a tight crimson sweater.

Shorts in the day, jeans at night. All the Boiling River locals knew the desert would freeze you as fast as cook you.

When she reached the start of Main Street, Claire shoved her hands into her pockets and ducked her head. The street was filling up fast, tourists spilling out of their hotels as the locals finished work and went to make some bad decisions.

She could hardly judge. This was monumentally dumb, but here she was, striding through town like she was being reeled on a fishing line. She even paused partway, hovering on the sidewalk before cursing under her breath and darting into the deli before it shut for the night.

The glass bottle in her hand was wet with condensation when she stepped back outside and kept walking. The receipt crinkled accusingly in her back pocket. She tried to ignore it.

The radio station's door was propped open with a brick. So much for the werewolf's precious territory, she thought sourly, stepping over the brick and squeezing inside. He didn't even bother to shut his station's door. Any weirdo—her included—could wander in off the street.

The station was quiet as she hurried through the halls. It was like last time: eerily empty. But the On Air sign glowed red above the recording studio's door, and Claire took a deep breath then gripped the handle.

She pushed the door open, flinching when the hinges creaked.

"Hi," she whispered, waving awkwardly as Zacharias stared at her from behind the glass divider. A rock ballad hummed through the speakers, quiet enough to hear the drag of the door over the carpet. Claire shut the door gently behind her and turned, holding the glass bottle behind her back.

"Hello," Zacharias said flatly. He did not look pleased to see her. A crease formed between his eyebrows as he looked at her, eyes darkening. "What do you want?"

Claire hid her wince. Yep. This was stupid.

"Nothing," she rasped, her sluggish mind desperately searching for an excuse.. "I was... in the area... and thought I'd say hi. On my way somewhere else."

Zacharias' mouth flattened. He was unconvinced. Claire shrugged and forced a smile, aiming for breezy but falling somewhere closer to manic.

"Anyway! That's done, so. I'll see you around." She spun and snatched for the door handle.

"Wait."

He didn't shout. Didn't raise his voice. The vampire was cool as his command surged through her. Claire froze, not because of some spell or some glamor, but because her treacherous body wanted to stay.

"What do you have there?" Zacharias stood, cocking his head as he peered through the divider. The glass bottle shook in her grip. It was too late to hide it, to pretend it was nothing. Claire cleared her throat, a flush prickling over her cheeks.

"A gift."

"For who?"

"For you." She spat the words, unable to decide who she was angrier with. Him, for his condescending coolness after spending the day in her home, or her, for expecting anything else. She'd worried about him for hours, she'd spoken for him to the police, she'd brought this stupid peace offering, and she'd forgotten who she was dealing with. *What* she was dealing with.

It suited him to charm her when she was saving his afterlife.

It didn't suit him anymore.

"Enjoy." She stalked to the nearest table and slammed the bottle down, glaring as it wobbled on its rim. Then she turned on her heel, not looking at Zacharias York, and pushed through the door back into the hallway.

How many times was she going to make a fool of herself over this vampire? How many times would she humiliate herself before learning her lesson?

No more—that was for sure. Claire Ramsden was *done*. A husky voice couldn't make up for a shitty personality. She should never have come here again, whatever trouble Zacharias York was tangled up in.

It was someone else's problem. His problem.

And he was nothing to her.

Chapter Twelve

*I*f Zacharias had thought being questioned over his doorman's attack and gaining a violent reputation would lessen his fan mail… he was sorely mistaken. Turned out, his fans loved that there was a good chance Zacharias was unhinged. That he was just as bloodthirsty as the worst of his kind..

It made him dangerous, sexy, predatory—the sort of vampire, they wrote eagerly, that might stalk them through the streets and climb in through their bedroom windows.

Zacharias scoffed, tossing the latest page of warped ramblings on top of the pile growing on his desk. He shouldn't have read them again. He'd ignored them for days, but a shameful part of him had been curious.

He'd wanted to see if anyone out there had faith in him. To see if anyone thought him innocent.

This was so much worse. Not only did they all think he'd done it, they were *thrilled*. Driven even more wild with lust.

Gods-damned humans. No self-preservation instincts.

"Everyone loves you, York. You can stop huffing now."

Angie prodded at the plant pot teetering on her desk. She'd been fussing over the spider plant since they'd discovered their wrecked office, gluing shards of the ceramic pot back in place and patting down the tossed soil. The pink tip of her tongue poked between her teeth, and her sleek black hair tickled at her shoulders as she leaned forwards, concentrating.

"This is not love," Zacharias ground out, sliding the pile over to Angie. "You'd think a cupid would know the difference."

Angie's eyebrow quirked, but she ignored the papers, dabbing at the leaves with a folded tissue. "Admiration, then."

"No."

It shouldn't rile him up this much, but he was so sick of everyone constantly misunderstanding him. Zacharias did not want admiration for supposedly attacking an old man. He did not want his office mate to reassure him that his crazy fans still loved him.

He wanted to be left the hell alone. With no fan mail and no questions from the cops.

"Here." He grabbed the back of Angie's chair, spinning her around to face his desk. He shoved the papers closer again, and though she glared at him, she spread her hand over the stack.

He watched as the color drained from her face.

"Oh."

Yes. *Oh.*

Angie shivered, snatching her hand back and cradling it against her chest. She sounded faintly sick when she spoke.

"That's an ugly kind of love."

"Indeed."

Angie cast a desperate glance around his desk, her gaze falling on the empty glass bottle now holding his pens. Her expression softened, and she let out a pleased sigh, leaning over to grab the bottle.

"Get rid of those." She prodded his fan letters with her elbow. "Focus on *this*."

Zacharias did not want to focus on his gift from Claire Ramsden. It was the worst sort of sentimentality, and he should never have kept a memento. He'd told himself it was because the blood she'd brought him was so delicious, he wanted to remember the brand.

"A pen holder," he said flatly. Angie huffed, blowing chin-length strands of dark hair out of her face.

"Don't play the fool."

Zacharias pushed to his feet, his gut churning with a sickly cocktail of emotions. The fan letters had left him feeling ill, grimy all over, but beneath that, guilt and regret squirmed inside him. He knew that Claire had confirmed his alibi. That she'd defended him to the Boiling River police, then brought him this gift. And in return, he'd brushed her off like lint from his sleeve.

He was more monstrous than he liked to admit.

Zacharias grabbed the wastepaper basket and swept the stack of fan mail and Claire's glass bottle into the trash. Then he turned and strode from the office without a word. He didn't want to think about this anymore.

He was in such a foul mood, his skin prickling and his fangs jabbing into his lower lip, that he didn't notice Yelena until he'd already barrelled into her. She stumbled back, wavering on her heels, arms pinwheeling in the center of the lobby.

"Sorry," Zacharias grunted, grabbing her narrow shoulder and steadying her on her feet. Apparently it was all the opening she needed—the podcaster launched into a stream of questions.

"Zach, hi! I was just looking for you. Have the police made any progress on your doorman's attack? Who do you think did it? Where were you when it happened? Are there many supernatural attacks in Boiling River?"

She held a recorder up as she spoke, her knuckles going white as her grip tightened. Still afraid of him, then. Good. And yet she felt she could call him *Zach*.

"No comment," he grumbled, trying to step around her. That was what people said, right? When they wanted a reporter to piss off? She wasn't a real reporter, and he wasn't a real criminal, but they could make do.

Yelena side-stepped neatly to block his path. Her eyes were wide and frightened, her pupils dilated, but her pink mouth was set in a firm line. The recorder trembled in her hand as she thrust it in his face.

"Is it true you have an alibi? That you spent the day of the attack with a local woman?"

Zacharias ground his fangs together. "That's nobody's business."

"And is it serious with this woman? Are supernatural-human relationships common in Boiling River?"

"There's a cupid down the hall." He jabbed a finger over Yelena's shoulder. "Why don't you ask her?"

He was being rude, he knew it, but this Yelena woman was like a terrier yapping at his ankles. Asking him about Claire, about poor Giles' attack, assuming he did it the same as everyone else—

Zacharias gripped Yelena by the shoulders, lifted her off the carpet, turned and thumped her back down. Then he turned and strode out of the station doors, back into the shadows of the night.

* * *

Claire Ramsden was not in her bungalow. Nor was she in the Silver Bullet, or Hex Mex, or any of the late night eateries. Zacharias prowled around the town, nostrils flaring as he caught faded wisps of her scent.

She must be here somewhere. A person didn't just disappear without a trace and without any kind of uproar. And Claire Ramsden was loved; she had friends and neighbors who cared about her, who'd notice if she was gone.

No. She was here somewhere, and he'd find her. The predator tucked deep inside Zacharias growled in approval.

He reached the end of Main Street, having walked the full length of the town. He'd been everywhere, tipping his face to scent the air, keeping to the darkest shadows and alleys. A thought occurred to him—an image of Claire with another man, tucked away in one of these houses.

Zacharias clenched his fists so hard the bones creaked.

Please, no. Anything but that.

It was none of his business, he knew that, and he'd never presume to tell Claire Ramsden who to date. But that didn't stop his instincts from raging beneath his skin; didn't stop his fangs from lengthening and his eyesight sharpening. He quickened his pace, leaving Main Street behind and striding back towards her bungalow.

As he neared the cluster of adobe cottages, her scent grew stronger. And when he stood at the end of her garden path, he caught a taste of something he'd missed earlier.

Her scent drifted away from the town, heading out across the bare desert. He'd been so set on finding her inside Boiling River, he'd missed her trail leading away from all buildings.

Very well. He could play hide and seek. Zacharias glanced up at the night sky yawning wide above, the mass of stars spinning slowly around the mountains. He had plenty of time. He set his feet to Claire's trail and walked on.

Tourists were forever warned about the dangers of wandering in the desert. There was the sun, obviously, the risk of heat stroke or worse, but there were also rattlesnakes and scorpions and mountain lions which stole on silent paws into the valley. Ant hills erupted out of the dirt, home to blood-red carnivorous insects, and malevolent spirits shrieked through cracks in the ground, calling wanderers to their fate. The ground was uneven, pockmarked with ditches and boulders, and if you were far enough away from town, a broken ankle could mean death.

But apparently Claire Ramsden fancied a midnight stroll.

Zacharias huffed a laugh, his chest easing now that he'd located her. Perhaps he should be more worried—should be scanning the ground for her rumpled form—but Claire was Boiling River born and bred. She knew the valley like she knew her own garden. She'd be just fine.

Her trail led between boulders and wove through towering cactus plants. They stood proud, silhouetted like men against the stars, and now and then, her scent would linger on their spines where she'd brushed her fingertips. It was like she was teasing him, dropping a breadcrumb trail, daring him to find her.

Zacharias swallowed hard, a drumbeat pounding in his ancient chest.

The river the town was named for snaked down one side of the valley. It lived up to its promise, the water churning hot, with steam floating up like mist towards the dark sky. Only a few of the supernaturals could bear the heat of the water, and even fewer of them enjoyed it. Claire, meanwhile, sat on the bank, her arms wrapped around her knees as she watched the chalky, simmering water. Her red hair splayed over her shoulders, and her overalls were streaked with dried clay.

"Moon-bathing?" Her head whipped around when he spoke, a stream of emotions flashing across her face. Surprise, pleasure, confusion, anger. "I didn't take you for a witch."

Claire's eyes narrowed. "What I am is none of your business."

She was human—he could smell it on her—but he didn't say so. She was already spitting mad at him, and he didn't track her all the way out here to piss her off even more.

"I'm sorry, Claire." His voice rumbled over the rush of the river. "I was an ass."

"Yes, you were."

"Thank you for the gift."

She snorted. "You're no longer welcome."

He couldn't blame her. She'd saved his hide again and again, and he'd repaid her with rudeness. His mother would turn in her grave, he mused ruefully. He hadn't thought of his mother in such a long time.

"You could have kept it."

"I don't have much use for blood."

He smirked, and his fangs prodded his lip. Her gaze dropped to their flash of pearly white, and he heard her breath come faster.

"You could paint with it."

Claire hummed. "Bit of a waste." She was still staring at his mouth, and if he didn't try for this now, it would haunt him all the way home. Zacharias strode forward to where she sat on the bank, and dropped to one knee beside her in the dirt.

His thumb tingled from the warmth of her as he stroked it over her cheekbone, and she gave the most delicious shiver in response. Her scent was everywhere, all around him, and he sucked in a chestful of her.

"You smell good enough to eat."

She rolled her eyes even as her fingers gripped his black shirt. "Does that line actually work on anyone?"

"You tell me."

Claire grumbled under her breath, the tang of her annoyance still clinging to her scent. But she yanked on her fistful of his shirt, tugging his face closer.

"Don't let this go to your head," she told him, her breath washing over his lips. He smiled—it felt like his first real smile in days—and pressed his lips gently to hers.

Sweetness. That was the first clear thought in his head. She tasted so gods-damned sweet. Her breath, her soft lips, even her scent—she was like the ice cream-blood floats in the diner. He groaned, slanting his mouth to deepen the kiss, drawing her tighter into his arms. And she gasped and arched into his touch, like she wanted him just as much.

Screw gentle. This woman was not made of glass. Zacharias dropped to the dirt, gathering Claire and pulling her into his lap. She straddled his hips, grinding down against him without any urging. And she wound her fingers into his dark hair, kissing him fiercely, like she was claiming him too.

She could have him. He was a fool, and he was already hers.

He'd been hers since the first time he laid eyes on her, but he'd been too damn stubborn to see it. But now, with her rocking against him, groaning into mouth, curling her tongue around his fangs—

He'd never go back. He was just enough of a bastard to keep

her.

A coyote howled somewhere in the distance, but neither of them tried to break apart. What was scarier out here in the desert than him? Claire tugged his shirt up and traced a hand over his abs. They contracted under her touch, his blood singing with need, the heat of her center positioned exactly over his cock. His every instinct screamed at him to tear off her clothes, to bury himself inside her and bite down on her throat.

Correction: what was scarier out here than Claire Ramsden, and the effect she had on him?

Zacharias forced his hands off her, fisting them at his sides. He let her grind against him and use him, kissing her back hard, but he kept his hands to himself.

There would be time enough for everything else. By the gods, he'd make sure there was time. But he refused to rush her, to give into base instinct, instead letting her ride out her pleasure. His head tipped back, and he gazed at the blurry stars as she sucked a bruise onto his throat.

She'd be the death of him. But what a delicious way to die.

Chapter Thirteen

Zacharias York was in her kitchen. Again.

He was rifling through her cupboards, the nosiest house guest Claire had ever had, unscrewing the caps of her instant coffee and cocoa powder, sniffing and wrinkling his nose.

"There's no blood in there." He glanced at her over his shoulder, a dark curl falling in his eyes. She shivered, pressing her thighs together, and gripped onto the kitchen counter to keep from tackling him to the floor.

There had been enough of that by the river. Hours spent lost in each other, clinging together and swaying on the bank, breathing as one. They needed to spend more than a few minutes apart—she needed space to *think*.

And all thoughts flew out of her brain when Zacharias York looked at her like that.

"If you're thirsty you'll have to order again."

His gaze dropped to the column of her throat, to the flush creeping up her chest.

"I'm very thirsty," he said darkly. Goosebumps erupted over her skin, but he sighed and pulled out his cell phone. He tapped away at the screen, no doubt ordering another ridiculous keg, and Claire turned to watch the sky bruise pink from the sunrise. A rare cloud drifting over the mountain peaks, lit gold from beneath. She wrapped her fingers around the cord for the window blind, ready to plunge them into darkness.

"Leave it."

Claire raised an eyebrow at the vampire prodding the bag of sugar by her coffee pot. You'd think he'd never been human from the fascinated way he picked through her things.

But maybe it wasn't curiosity for how humans lived. Maybe it was just about her.

"Hm. You don't seem suicidal, York."

He slid her a look out of the corner of his eye, rearranging the apples on her fruit bowl.

"First vamp, now York. Will you ever call me Zacharias?"

"Perhaps." She grinned at him. "If I'm ever truly desperate."

His gaze darkened and he stepped forward, as if to test that theory, but the sun burst over the horizon.

Zacharias dropped to his knees in front of her just as sunlight spilled through the kitchen window. He smirked at her, curling his hands around the back of her thighs, and nudged her feet apart.

"I'll have to take shelter down here," he said sadly. "Whatever will I do to pass the time?"

Claire bit back a grin, stepping her feet wider and sucking in a breath as he slid his palms over her overalls. He stroked around her waist, up to her mid back, lingering to fiddle with the buckles from her shoulder straps. Then he sat back on his heels and scowled at her outfit.

"How the hell do you get these bastard clothes off? Tell me, woman." Claire wheezed from laughter, collapsing back against the counter as Zacharias tugged at her pockets. "These infernal denim contraptions. When I rule the world, they'll be banned on pain of death."

"Bit harsh," Claire spluttered, bursting into giggles as Zacharias growled and buried his face between her legs, denim and all. She reached down, winding her fingers through his hair, when a knock at her back door made them jump apart. A man stood in her garden, his broad shoulders fuzzy through the frosted glass.

"Danny," Claire muttered. She recognized the messy tawny hair and blue police officer's uniform. "Hang on." She reached over and tugged on the blind, filling the kitchen with shadows. Zacharias pushed to his feet, irritation rolling off him in waves. He crossed his arms, planted his feet, and glared at the back door.

"I'll get it then, shall I?" Claire grumbled, stomping to the door and spinning the key in the lock. When the door swung open, the spicy scent of the desert washed inside.

"Miss Ramsden." The leopard shifter nodded at her formally. Claire sighed.

"We've known each other twenty years, Danny."

The officer's jaw tightened, but he said nothing, frowning over her shoulder. Behind her, Zacharias lounged against the counter, tossing a green apple in one palm.

"To what do we owe the pleasure, officer?" he drawled, and Claire bristled at him acting like he ruled her bungalow. He was a guest, a visitor, no matter how many of her jars he sniffed. She cleared her throat, waiting until Danny looked back to her before she lifted her chin.

"What's going on, Danny?"

The leopard shifter twisted his mouth, his brown eyes wary as they landed back on Zacharias.

"I'm actually here for him, Claire. There's been another incident at his building."

If it bothered Zacharias to hear them discuss him like he wasn't there, Claire couldn't bring herself to care. He shouldn't have bristled up like a tom cat defending his territory. She was a grown woman in her own home, and this was the twenty-first century for gods' sake.

"What happened? Was there another attack?" Zacharias shifted behind her, his boots scraping over the tiles.

"No…" Danny stretched out the word. There was something he wasn't telling. Finally, he sighed, jerking his chin at Zacharias. "You'd better come and see."

"Of course." Zacharias prowled forward, his words clipped. "I'll come at once. Will you carry my ashes in your pocket or would you like to borrow some Tupperware from Claire?"

Danny's nostrils flared, his eyes flashing gold, but he reined his temper in, clasping his hands behind his back. Behind him, Mabel craned over their shared garden fence, trying desperately to eavesdrop. Her multicolored shawls snagged on the wood, and her sunglasses slid to the very tip of her nose.

"Fine. We'll send a squad car for you at dusk."

"How exciting," Zacharias said, tone withering. Danny turned on his heel, nodding to Mabel as he marched down the mosaic path. The old banshee raised a hand and screamed.

When Zacharias turned back to Claire, all his earlier humor was gone. His eyes were hard, his jaw clenched, and his hands were shoved in his pockets.

Another long day in her bungalow together.

Fun.

* * *

"You can't brood for the whole day." Claire stumbled through the door with a comforter wrapped around her shoulders. She'd excused herself for a nap—gods, she needed to get more sleep, she was turning into Olivia—and four hours later, when she tracked him down in her studio, Zacharias still wore the same sour expression.

"Yes, I can." He flicked an eraser on her workstation. "I've had two hundred years of practice."

"Impressive," she purred, dropping her comforter and crossing to where he stood in the corner. He'd drawn the curtains, a broom handle abandoned on the floor, and her usually cheerful studio was now a den of vampish misery. The half-done paintings stacked against the walls were cloaked in shadows, and the only light in the room came from the table lamp on her desk.

When Claire slid her arms around the vampire's waist and pressed her cheek to his back, she heard the slowed down thump of his heart.

"I didn't think you had a pulse."

His voice was bitter over her head. "Why, because I'm heartless?"

"No. Because you're undead, you ass."

Zacharias shrugged, his shoulder blades shifting under her cheek. "I don't need it. But it's uncomfortable otherwise. Same with breathing."

Claire traced a pattern on the back of his shirt. "What's the longest you've gone without breathing?"

"Months," he said immediately. "I came to the US on the Titanic in 1912. Or partway, at least. When it sank, I had to swim the rest of the way, and breathing became a bother."

Claire stared at her studio wall, processing.

The Titanic. 1912. Swimming to the US. Breathing became a *bother*.

"Did you see sharks? Did they attack you? Why didn't you mention that in your podcast interview? That's crazy!"

Zacharias grunted. "It didn't come up. And of course there were sharks. What else would I drink?"

Uh-uh. Sure. Of course.

"Why didn't you get in a lifeboat?"

"I didn't fit the criteria," Zacharias said dryly.

This was... a lot. Incredibly cool, yes, and already ideas for drawings and paintings were filling her brain, but Claire had never felt the small scale of her existence quite so harshly before. She was born in this desert valley; she went to school here and now she sold paintings and visited Dad and hung out with her friends.

It was a far cry from the Titanic in 1912. Claire slid her arms back from the vampire's waist, stepping away.

Zacharias turned and watched her go, a resigned expression on his face.

They were so different. In every conceivable way. He was grumpy and growly and preferred to be alone. She was bright mosaic tiles and vivid paints, and loneliness stole her breath away when she thought about living in this bungalow without Dad.

Zacharias drank blood.

Claire drank bad instant coffee.

They had nothing at all to talk about.

Claire cleared her throat, embarrassed at the silence hanging thick between them. She wished she hadn't been so quick to drop her comforter; goosebumps had prickled over her arms. But she couldn't turn away now; it would seem like a retreat. A rejection.

"What would you like to do today?"

She watched as Zacharias' face twitched with the effort not to roll his eyes.

"What delights do you have hidden in your bungalow?"

Claire bristled at his sarcasm, but pushed on. "There are books and art supplies and you can watch stuff on my laptop, or of course you can carry on being a complete ass," she finished as the vampire turned away from her mid-sentence. He strolled around the edge of the studio, hands tucked in his pockets. "Do you have to be so freaking rude?"

"I'll watch you work," he said, ignoring her completely.

Claire blew a strand of hair out of her face.

"I didn't offer that."

"Because your paintings are top secret? You didn't mind last time."

"Because I'm working on a landscape and you've drawn the curtains."

"The sun was shining inside."

Claire pressed the heel of her palms into her eye sockets. By rights, this should be easier. They'd kissed, they'd spent hours wrapped around each other at the riverbank. But somehow, Danny's visit had set them back ten steps. They were back to the surly vampire and exasperated artist, both irritated by their mutual attraction.

"I'll draw you." Claire dropped her hands. "If you want to watch, you have to model."

Surprise flickered over Zacharias' face, followed by wry amusement.

"If you wanted me to take my clothes off, you need only ask."

Claire actually *growled*. At this rate, she'd stake him well before sunset.

* * *

"Hold still."

Zacharias shifted on the foam mattress Claire had laid out on the floor. He was shirtless—she'd stopped him there, mouth already dry—and his dark hair was pulled free from its tie, tumbling over his broad shoulders. Beside him, an ancient heater rattled on the floor, glowing red inside its metal cage. He'd insisted the heater was unnecessary, that he couldn't get cold, but she felt better this way.

"You're a terrible model," she murmured, sketching the slope of his shoulder. Zacharias raised a hand to scratch his cheek, winking at her when she dropped her charcoal to glare.

"A poor artist blames her tools."

"Is that what you are?" Claire asked mildly, sketching again. "A tool?"

"Undoubtedly."

He was better than she gave him credit for, really. He'd let her position him like a mannequin, propped up on one elbow, heat flushing up her neck as she'd touched his bare skin. He hadn't even teased her when she'd traced her fingertips over the dark hair dusting his chest, lying still and silent for her perusal.

The heater cast an orange glow over the vampire's body, and for once he almost looked tanned. He lay there, watching her just as intently as she watched him, and her blood thrummed through her body as she sketched.

"Have you done this before?"

Zacharias snorted from the mat, and it was such an undignified sound Claire grinned.

"I'm not in as high demand as you seem to think."

"Really? I heard you have quite the fan club for your radio show."

Zacharias shifted again. "Where did you hear that?"

Claire shrugged. "I was thinking about joining." She shot him a smirk over the top of her sketchpad, but he wasn't smiling. He frowned over her shoulder, his gaze far away. "I won't join now, of course," she said brightly, dragging his attention back to her. "Not now I've seen you shirtless."

"Not up to scratch?" A smile tugged the corner of his mouth, and Claire let out a relieved breath.

"Hideous. Sorry."

His laugh was low and rumbling. It reminded Claire of the rock slides that sometimes echoed down the valley: deep and full of distant power. She shivered, biting her bottom lip as she sketched the line of his waist. It was easier, now, being around him. Like she'd been inoculated somehow. She felt less like she was about to lose her mind and hump his leg, and more like a sane, rational human.

Zacharias still did things to her, though. His voice. His dark eyes. Hell, even his scent when she'd been close enough to breathe it. But she'd finally come to accept that it wasn't a glamor. It was just him. She squirmed on her seat, pressing her thighs together.

"I've heard in some art classes, the models move around." He was staring at her again, voice rough.

Claire licked her lips. "Do you need to stretch your legs?"

Zacharias fastened his gaze on her throat. "Desperately."

He surged to his feet, and she realized distantly that she must have nodded. He crossed to her chair in three strides and plucked the lump of charcoal from her trembling fingers before tossing it to the floor.

"I could smell your arousal from over there." He dropped to his knees, nudging her legs apart. Claire frowned, not sure she liked that revelation. She tried to close her thighs again, but he pressed them apart, gentle but firm. "Don't be embarrassed. You smell delicious."

"And you're a pervert," Claire ground out, but she let her legs fall wide. Zacharias ran his palms up the tops of her thighs, over her ancient blue overalls. He growled as he prodded his fingertips inside the pockets and creases, searching for a zipper or button.

"One day, I will come to you and you won't be dressed as a puzzle box."

Claire's laugh sounded like a hiccup. "Don't hold your breath."

"Oh." He leaned close, eyes flicking over her bright cheeks, her heaving chest. "I intend to."

And how could Claire ignore a promise like that? She scrabbled at the buckles of her shoulder straps, tugging them undone, then pushed the fabric to her waist. She wore a thin white t-shirt below, but no bra, and her nipples stood out beneath the cotton.

Zacharias frowned at her chest, his hands fastened on her waist, and his hum reverberated through his fingertips straight to her bones. Then he leaned forward, the t-shirt still maddeningly in place, and licked a stripe over one nipple. It grew even harder under his attention, straining forward to meet him as the white cotton turned translucent.

"Gods." Claire's head rolled back on her shoulder and she stared up at the ceiling. Her fingers played in the vampire's long hair. A sharp pinch made her gasp, and she looked down again to find Zacharias watching her, her nipple held between his teeth.

"Shit." She squirmed in her chair, and he bit down the tiniest amount. Heat flooded her core, she was burning up, she couldn't breathe—

Zacharias released her nipple and switched to her other breast, repeating the same attentions on her other side. Claire watched him this time, wide eyes glued on him as he took her nipple between his fangs. His tongue swept out, teasing the tip, and she tugged on his hair, desperate for more. More of what, exactly, she didn't know, but she'd die unless she found out soon. Zacharias hummed again, a soothing noise, and leaned back to tug her t-shirt over her head.

"Now we're even." He winked at her, and seeing him light and playful like this was like seeing a different man. He palmed her breast, squeezing and kneading it, and if his cold skin was a shock at first, it also sent a shudder through her core.

"Don't play favorites," Claire gasped, and he obediently took her other breast in hand too. He lavished attention over her chest, her shoulders, his fangs scraping over the column of her throat. Never biting, though, and the thought never crossed Claire's mind to be scared.

"You can bite me if you want," she murmured, dazed from his attentions. "You can drink from me."

Zacharias sat back on his heels and gave her a rueful smile.

"Another time, sweetheart. When I'm more in control."

He seemed in control now, infuriatingly so, each movement of his measured and precise. He drew sighs and whimpers from her like a musician playing an instrument, and all she could do was hold on to his shoulders for dear life. Claire scowled at the thought—she wouldn't be just another conquest—and shoved the vampire away.

"What's wrong?" he asked immediately, but she kept pushing until he sat on the ground, then slid off her chair to straddle his legs. Her fingers were clumsy as she undid his buttons and tugged down his fly. She paused, glancing up to find his eyes burning into her.

"Yes?"

"Yes."

He was cold in her palm, and she didn't know what else she expected. His skin slid under her grip as she gave an experimental tug, and the grunt that slipped out of him was so delicious. When was the last time he'd ceded control? When was the last time someone brought him undone? Claire ran her thumb over the tip of him, and his whole body shuddered beneath her thighs.

Yes. This was more like it.

His flattened palm smoothed over her bare back as she shuffled back on her knees and leaned forwards. Claire reached behind her and grabbed his wrist, then placed his hand in her hair. He took the hint, gathering her coppery strands and holding them out of her way. Then he watched her, a pained frown etched on his face as she took him in her mouth.

It had been a while since she'd done this, but Zacharias clearly didn't mind. Whatever Claire lacked in practice, she apparently made up for with her shameless enthusiasm. She groaned around him, bobbing her head and hollowing her cheeks like she could suck out what was left of his soul. And when she felt his spare hand creep along her stomach and dip under her waistband, she spread her legs to welcome him inside.

They might fight half the time they spent together. They might drive each mad. But here, they were in complete understanding, moving together like they'd been practicing for years. They fell into the same rhythm, and climbed together towards the same peak. Zacharias' breaths came fast, his muscles tightening under her just as the dip and slide of his fingers brought her to the edge. Claire moaned around him, the spasms starting in her core and rippling out through the rest of her body. And Zacharias fell too, letting out a husky groan and tugging her hair to warn her before spilling in her mouth. She grasped his hips and held him to her, not letting him slide away, her thumbs rubbing circles on his skin.

Her ears rang. Claire sat back on her heels, the studio quiet except for the rattling heater and their gasping breaths.

"Well," Zacharias said finally, his voice hoarse. "That's one way to pass the time."

Claire smacked his leg, a grin stretching her aching cheeks, and pushed her hair out of her eyes.

It was one way, definitely. One of many, if she had anything to say about it.

Chapter Fourteen

*T*he trill of Claire's front doorbell made Zacharias stiffen. He'd forgotten about the police officer's visit this morning. He'd been so wrapped up in Claire, his mind wiped blissfully clean since the moment she popped open his top button, that he'd failed to brood all day as planned.

Claire sighed from his lap. Her head rested on his thighs, his fingers carding through her coppery hair as they chatted amiably about childhoods and hobbies and other sweet nonsense. The doorbell shattered their newfound peace, and Claire groaned as she sat up, rolling her head on her neck like she'd had a hard day of labor.

Well. He'd made her sweat, at least.

"Freaking Danny," Claire grumbled, like it was the leopard shifter's fault somehow that Zacharias was required elsewhere. It was possible there had been another attack, he mused, and Zacharias was wanted for questioning. Or perhaps there'd been another break in at the station. He slid Claire a smirk.

"Is there anything you'd like to tell me before we speak to

the nice officer?"

The look she gave him was so dirty, he bit down on his lip to keep from laughing.

"If someone's trashed your office again, I guarantee you deserve it."

"Almost certainly." Zacharias traced a fingertip down Claire's bare arm as she slid her overall straps back over her shoulders. Fully dressed, she pushed off the sofa and crammed her feet into her worn sneakers.

"What?" She frowned when she caught his hesitant expression. "Don't you want me to come?"

It came out like a challenge, but he'd be a fool to miss the vulnerability behind her green eyes. He joined her by the door, holding her elbow as she hopped on one leg and tugged her sneaker the rest of the way on.

"Of course you should come. You're my alibi."

It was the wrong thing to say. She huffed a laugh, but it was bitter. Resigned. And though Zacharias opened his mouth to take it back, to undo it somehow, Claire was already turning the lock and stepping outside.

It was odd, leaving by the front door. It seemed formal. Ceremonial. The scuff line of his keg still trailed through the dirt in a wobbly line to the front step. Zacharias walked it like a tightrope to the idling squad car.

"Daniel." He nodded at the officer in the front seat, smirking at the flash of irritation. Then he slid into the backseat of the car, his chest tight until Claire sat beside him.

He wasn't completely unpopular, then. She still wanted him near, even when he was an ass.

The drive across Boiling River was barely worth the effort. So many tourists and locals strode down the center of Main

Street, laughing and carousing, that the car crawled behind at a walking pace.

"The horn is a wonderful invention," Zacharias spat after fifteen minutes. They should have arrived at the radio station by now. And he shouldn't brood like this, shouldn't be such a moody bastard, but the four inches of space between Claire and his side set him on edge. He was crotchety, unsure of himself and pissed off at her, at himself, at damned Officer Daniel for the whole situation.

"The radio station's that way." Zacharias pointed to the turning as they drove past, inching along with plenty of time to turn the corner. He blew out a breath as they continued down the Main Street. Not a work problem, then.

The image of his elderly doorman's bloodied head made him sit forward, hand gripping on to the seat in front.

"Is someone hurt? Is it Giles?" The old codger was still in hospital, but perhaps it hadn't been a random attack or bungled burglary. Perhaps it was personal.

"Your doorman is fine," the police officer muttered, craning forward to peer at the darkened road. As the final rays of daylight faded, the crowds moving in front of the car became shadows, lit only by headlights.

"What's the issue, then?" Zacharias urged, impatient, but the officer was done talking. He fixed his narrowed eyes on the road, his mouth pressed in a firm line, and guided the car through the streets.

"This is ridiculous." Zacharias turned to Claire, but she was staring out of the window, lost in thought. A faint crease marred her forehead, and she chewed on her bottom lip.

Perfect.

First the police; now even Claire thought him suspicious.

Even though they'd spent the night together, even though just hours ago, she'd trusted him enough to do *that*. It stung more than he'd thought it would, a vicious slice through his chest, and Zacharias gritted his teeth and stared out his own window.

This was why he didn't get involved. Didn't date. People were fickle; painful and temporary.

And *homes* were no better. The word barely held meaning for him anymore.

For a long time, home had been the north of England, where his family worked and fought and loved. It was the cramped terraced house his parents rented, with two bedrooms to house ten. Even long after his change, when his siblings grew old and passed, Zacharias thought of that house as home. And once he left, everywhere else he lived was a convenience. Nothing more.

He'd made the crucial mistake, though. With Boiling River, he'd gotten attached. He'd forgotten his hard-won lessons from two hundred years as a vampire, and put down roots.

He'd hung paintings on the wall. Ordered his bookshelves. Even brought in some dark-loving plants. Zacharias had grown foolishly attached to his underground apartment, and as Officer Daniel led them through his building's lobby, a hard stone of dread settled in his gut.

Zacharias knew before the officer summoned the elevator which button he would press. And he evaded Claire's worried eyes as they piled inside and sank down to his floor.

"Is this your place?" she asked in a whisper.

Zacharias did not reply.

The mess from his office was nothing compared to the wreckage on the other side of the elevator doors. His furniture was torn to pieces, shards of wood and cushion stuffing littering the stone tiles. Black dye stained his pool; his paintings were ripped from their frames. He glanced at Claire when he saw that—it must be shocking to see, as an artist, like seeing your own work destroyed—but she stared around with wide eyes and pale cheeks.

He couldn't blame her. It was almost dazzling to know someone loathed him this much.

The plants smashed in their pots, their soil scattered and roots bared—that was the worst part. It was Angie's desk plant all over again, but she wasn't here to re-pot them and wipe down their leaves. No; these plants only had him, and already Zacharias could feel the chill spreading through his chest.

He wouldn't save them. He didn't know how. He couldn't even save himself. Not when he turned to Claire Ramsden, took her elbow gently, and said: "Get out."

She frowned. "What? Why?" She stepped closer, her scent washing over him in the most delicious torture. Already, his fangs were cutting into his lip, his undead heart pounding out a beat for a chase. Anger thrummed through him, urging him towards violence, towards blood, and she couldn't be here. Not while he was like this.

"Get out," he ground out again. "I don't want you here." It was harsh, but he needed her to go. "I have to deal with this, and you'll only get in the way."

That did it. The confusion on her face bled away, replaced by cold anger. His chest ached, even as the predator deep inside him snarled with excitement.

"Fine," she said, voice clipped, then turned on her heel. "Bye, Danny," she threw over her shoulder.

Zacharias watched, chest heaving as she stepped back inside the elevator. He didn't warrant a goodbye, but the officer did?

Claire turned just as the doors closed, meeting his eye, her face turned to stone.

Fine. It was always headed for this, one way or another. He'd have liked more time, but this was probably better. This way he could walk away from her before he truly risked himself.

The police officer raised an eyebrow when Zacharias turned to face him, but he ignored him, grinding his fangs.

"What evidence have you found?" he asked, voice deadly. "Who did this? Show me."

* * *

Zacharias was knee-deep in a pile of torn books when his intercom buzzed. He frowned at the metal box on his wall, contemplating.

It could be Claire. Somehow, she might have looked past his worst nature and come back. He'd have to send her away again.

The intercom buzzed again, louder and longer this time, and Zacharias sighed and pushed to his feet. That was not a Claire Ramsden buzz. He didn't know whether he was more relieved or disappointed.

"What?" he barked into the microphone. Static crackled, then morphed into a laugh.

"See?" he heard a tinny voice murmur. "Told you so."

Zacharias thumped his forehead against the wall, breathing in hard through his nose. When he'd called Otis, he'd only meant to explain why he'd be missing his shift again. He'd expected a curt response. Frustration or anger. Not eager questions, and an offer to help with cleanup.

Zacharias lifted his head out of the dent he'd made in his wall, and pressed the intercom button again.

"I told you I don't need any help."

Someone murmured something in the background, and Otis roared with laughter. "Yeah," he said over the speaker, still chuckling. "Keep telling yourself that."

Zacharias could send them away. He'd made himself perfectly clear over the phone, and the last thing his gods-awful mood needed was that idiot werewolf laughing at his misfortune. Zacharias opened his mouth to tell them to leave, but pressed the unlock button instead.

Damned idiot. By the gods, he was a weak-minded fool.

Otis' mysterious companion turned out to be Angie, the tiny plump cupid striding out of the elevator behind the werewolf. She propped her rubber gloved hands on her hips, then sucked in a horrified breath when she saw the brutalized plants.

"Please." Zacharias waved at the mound of soil, suddenly glad the pair had come. "Do what you can for them."

Otis murmured something under his breath about *plants not people*, but he looked truly sorry as he scanned the apartment. He'd been here once before, knew how it looked whole, and his wide mouth turned down at the corners. The werewolf scratched his beard, the rasp loud in the cavernous wreckage, then gave Zacharias a nod.

"This will be a bitch," he announced, low and solemn, then wandered off towards the kitchen. He emerged moments later with a broom in one hand and a roll of trash bags in the other. Something clenched in Zacharias' icy chest, the tiniest thaw spreading through his gut.

Would Claire have grabbed a broom and set to work like that? Standing at his side without question?

Yes, he thought grimly. All the more reason to send her away.

Angie glanced at him from where she knelt among his pot

117

plants, as though she'd heard his thoughts. Perhaps it was a cupid thing; perhaps she could smell the pathetic yearning rising off him like mist.

"It's the same as your office," she said instead, passing a splayed rubber glove over the tangled leaves. "The ugly love."

Zacharias straightened an inch and strode to her, dropping to his knees like he too could sense something from the mess. This was more than that fool police officer had come up with, never mind his leopard senses. A *fan* did this to him.

An ugly kind of love indeed. Zacharias thought of Claire and rubbed his chest.

"Can you tell anything else? What do they look like? What species are they?"

Angie shook her head before he finished talking. She rubbed a waxy green leaf between her finger and thumb.

"That's all I've got. Sorry, Zacharias." She was so downcast. Like she'd failed him somehow. This sweet little cupid, who shared an office with his grumblings without a word of complaint. She'd dropped everything to come and help clean up his apartment, and now she was sorry for giving him the only lead he had.

Zacharias gripped the cupid's shoulder.

"Don't apologize, Angie." She gave a wobbly smile.

Zacharias squeezed her shoulder gently, then pushed to his feet. He strode into his kitchen to find another broom.

He'd never had people come to his aid like this before, even back as a human. It filled him with awkward, clunky gratitude. He didn't know what to do with it.

But first—he had a vandal to find.

Chapter Fifteen

*B*ree slammed a bottle of tequila onto the library check out desk. Claire had called her to rant as soon as she left Zacharias' building, not expecting anything more than a friendly ear, but Bree had declared all men were bastards and proclaimed tonight a *girls' night*.

Bree's girls' nights were legendary. Photo and video evidence of the carnage went viral online. Tales from girls' nights past were told in hushed whispers around bar tables. A few of the wilder stories were eternalized as footnotes in the tourists' guidebooks.

"Not my library," Olivia moaned, peeking between her fingers. She sat behind the desk, catching up on her work hours after closing time. Her apartment must be ankle deep in dust, Olivia went there so rarely these days. She cast a helpless look at Claire, leaning against the nearest stacks.

Claire shrugged. They both knew better. Bree was a force of nature; she could not be stopped.

"I offered my bungalow," she called, "but Bree wanted a

change."

"We always drink in your house," Bree threw over her shoulder. "It's sad. You get all mopey about your dad. Not tonight." She tossed a bag of limes onto the desk. "Tonight is a celebration. Claire-Bear dodged a bloodsucking bullet, and I won eighty bucks at poker."

Olivia's fingers clawed down her cheeks then dropped into her lap. She looked tired again, Claire noted. Worn thin. The purple shadows beneath her eyes had become a permanent feature, and her lips were pale.

"We don't have to, Liv," Claire said softly. She pushed away from the stacks and walked closer to the desk. "We could have a sleepover instead. Or go out for breakfast tomorrow."

Bree shot her a look of abject betrayal, but Claire widened her eyes. Bree cottoned on, turning a worried gaze on Olivia.

The librarian sank into her chair, a small, pale face in a sea of knitted sweater.

"Alright," she rasped from the depths of her layers, "I'm in. Stop looking at me like that."

"Like what?" Bree rummaged in her bag for a handful of salt packets.

"Like I'm some mental patient you have to tiptoe around. I'm not crazy." Olivia's hands were balled into fists in her lap, and two spots of color glowed on her cheeks.

"No one thinks that," Claire murmured, even though Olivia did look kind of unhinged. "You're just tired. That's all."

And how could she not be? Olivia hadn't slept through the night in months. She'd always been a light sleeper, even in school—the first to stir at their sleepovers. But lately, it was a sickness. She was fading away.

Olivia glared at her, then sagged. She looked so defeated,

Claire's chest ached.

"Don't hurt the books." She pulled a stack towards her, brushing salt packets off the top. "And don't set anything on fire."

Bree drew a cross over her generous chest. "Scouts' honor."

And since that was not the most reassuring promise, Claire helped tidy the last books off the desk. They tucked them beneath the table on the carpet, sliding the stacks well away from stray boots, and while she was down there in the darkness with Olivia, Claire whispered the question that burned her tongue.

"Have you seen it again? The ghost?"

Olivia let out a shuddery sigh.

"Always. I always see it."

This was the reason Olivia did not sleep; the reason she declared she wasn't crazy. Olivia saw ghosts. Or perhaps one ghost in particular; she didn't seem sure.

"Has it said anything?" Claire knew nothing about hauntings, but she figured it must want something to be hanging around like a bad smell. "Maybe we should go and see the witches at Starlight Springs."

"No." Olivia's voice was rough. "I'll handle it."

How? Claire wanted to ask, but she bit her tongue. Olivia was no witch; she hadn't handled it so far; but Claire said none of that. She nudged her friend's narrow shoulder with her own and told her: "I know you will."

It was a lie, but a pretty one. And hopefully, it would come true. Because although Olivia seemed the meek, quiet one of their group, she would not be pushed. Her bones were built from adamantium beneath those woolly sweaters.

It was just as well, Claire thought as she slid back out from under the desk. Bree was lining up shot glasses.

* * *

The havoc of girls' night was such a good distraction that Claire barely thought about Zacharias. He only crossed her mind when she had a second to think, or when she saw the stars through the window or had a space between breaths. She plastered a broad smile over her face, tossing back the drinks Bree passed her and giggling with Olivia at Bree's impressions of the tourists. And she managed not to scream, or punch a fist through the library wall, so Claire mentally patted herself on the back.

She'd fallen for it. She'd been sucked in, just like her gullible mother. She'd fallen for a vampire's charms—fallen for *him*. And he'd repaid her the way she'd always known he would: with callous indifference.

If it wasn't so pathetic, it might be funny.

"We should go to Hex Mex." Claire sat cross-legged on the library desk, surrounded by a halo of shredded salt packets. When she rocked side to side, the edges of her sneakers crunched in the fine layer of salt on the wood.

"Yup." Olivia lounged back in her chair, flicking a stapler. "Then someone else has to clean up."

Clean up. Claire's thoughts flew to Zacharias and his trashed apartment. Had he fixed it up yet? Was he still surrounded by the wreckage of his home? She screwed her eyes shut and breathed in through her nose.

No. She would not be this tragic. She would not be her mother. She'd shake this off like every other disappointment in life, and she would learn her damn lesson.

"Let's go." She swung her legs off the desk. "I want to dance."

The downside with walking the four blocks to Hex Mex was the frosty desert night. Claire shivered, wrapping her bare arms around herself, dressed only in her usual overalls and t-shirt. The cold was enough to sting her eyes and make her teeth ache, and by the time they reached the third block, she was most of the way back to sober.

Claire's stomach growled, but she kept her eyes on the street in front and absolutely did *not* look at the late night deli.

Bree and Olivia were still tipsy, both bundled in jackets, and they laughed together and linked arms as they marched down the street. Claire hurried to keep up, uncomfortably aware of her sore heart in her chest now that the alcohol was fading away.

Dancing. More drinks. She could do this. She could put on a brave face for her friends.

Then she could go back to her bungalow, bundle up in her comforter, and eat her body weight in chocolate fudge ice cream.

The troll bouncer outside the Hex Mex entrance gave them a stern look but stepped aside from the doorway. They spilled into the warmth, Claire rubbing at the goosebumps on her arms, and wound their way through the club's maze-like hallways.

It was a feature. The tourists loved it—the winking promise that if you wandered off in Hex Mex you might be lost for weeks. Of course, it was all fun and games until someone missed their bus home, but what did they expect?

This was Boiling River, an undead town in an undead valley. There were no empty threats.

"Drinks!" Bree yelled in Claire's ear over the distant, thumping bass. Claire nodded, hooking her finger through Bree's belt loop and letting her lead the way. The lights dimmed as they walked, the music grew louder, and the hallway opened up into a cavernous room. It was far too big to fit in this building—another of Hex Mex's secrets. Bree pushed through the surging crowd, heading straight for the bar, and Claire kept a tight hold on her belt loop until a firm chest stepped into her path.

Zacharias stood before her, frowning down at her with an unreadable expression. His hair was tied back again, a few curly strands escaping to hang around his face. He looked so gods-damned perfect, a walking work of art, and Claire was freaking sick of it.

"Excuse me." She moved to step around him, not even bothering to let him speak. What could he possibly have to say that she'd want to hear?

"You're out drinking," he said, voice flat. And he was such a damn hypocrite, judging her when he was here too, acting like he had a right to any opinion on the things she did. Claire's finger jabbed into his chest as she prowled forward, and he actually backed up a step.

"So are you, you gigantic asshole, and it's none of your damn business anyway. Leave. Me. Alone." She punctuated the last three words with extra vicious jabs.

"Claire," he said weakly, circling her wrist with a gentle grip, and she was the biggest fool in the world because she let him drag her back to the hallway. He led her through the maze of corridors, but rather than the exit, they stepped into a stairwell. Up and up they climbed, Claire's thighs burning and her brain screaming at her to tug her wrist free and leave, until finally Zacharias pushed through a doorway and led them out onto the roof.

"Gregor," Zacharias called out to the darkness, lit only by starlight. "Give us a minute."

On the corner of the building, a statue shifted, its stone limbs scraping over each other.

"I *live* here, man."

Zacharias sighed. "Please. You can use my roof."

The gargoyle grumbled to himself, but clambered over the side of the building.

"Is he okay?" Claire murmured. She should be used to Boiling River's gargoyles, but guilt still nipped at her insides for sending one off his roof. What if he slipped on the climb down? What if he fell, and when they stepped back onto the street they found a pile of rubble? What if—

"He's fine." Zacharias dropped her wrist and pointed to a dark shape scaling a building across the street. As they watched, he climbed with inhuman speed, then dashed across the roof and leaped to the neighboring townhouse.

Claire's heartbeat slowed as she watched the gargoyle go, the nip of guilt fading away in her gut. She took a deep, steadying breath, crossed her arms and turned to the vampire at her side.

"What do you want, Zacharias?"

She thought she saw his mouth turn down. It was hard to tell in the darkness, but her eyes were slowly adjusting to the gloom, and the vampire's pale skin seemed to absorb the starlight.

"I owe you an apology."

"And you needed to drag me up here for that?"

"I'm sorry, Claire."

"Great. Apology accepted." She turned to the doorway, to the slant of light spilling onto the roof, but his voice stopped her in her tracks. He sounded... raw. Pleading.

"Claire. Don't go just yet."

It was so freaking unfair of him to act upset. To be *hurt*, when he was the idiot who threw them off course. Claire wanted to pull his stupid hair, she wanted to push him off the roof, she wanted—

Claire pinched the bridge of her nose.

"What do you *want*, Zacharias?"

"You." He sounded so certain, but then, he'd sounded sure before. And he probably did want her, then and now, but he was fickle, a vampire, and he'd change his mind again before she knew it. But...

For all that was true, Claire couldn't deny the pounding of her pulse. The way her body came alive in his presence, her blood rushing and her nerves skittering under her skin. Perhaps she could do this his way, could live in the moment then cut all ties without a blink.

A one-night stand. Just like Bree told her eons ago. To get him out of her system.

"This means nothing," Claire whispered, stepping close to Zacharias. She wound her arms around his neck, waiting for his nod before she rocked up onto her toes.

"Alright," he rasped as she ran the freezing tip of her nose up his throat. It bobbed as he swallowed. "That's probably for the best."

For the best. Anger flooded through Claire's veins, sharpening her desire. She plunged her hands into his hair, gripping on tight, and dragged his mouth down to hers. She didn't care when his fangs scraped over her lip, drawing a hint of blood. She didn't care when Zacharias hardened against her, groaning and gathering her close. She gave back as good as she got, kissing and nipping, pulling on his hair.

"Quickly," she murmured against his lips, backing him up against the nearest wall. This was not a moment she wanted to linger in. It felt too good. It hurt too much.

She dragged her hands out of his hair and down his chest, grabbing two fistfuls of his sweater before swinging them around.

Zacharias' shoulders blocked out the starlight. He crowded her back against the cold brick, his thigh sliding between hers. Claire rocked against him, desperate for friction as her core throbbed, and fumbled with his belt.

"These damn overalls," Zacharias muttered, breaking their kiss to undo her straps, but she didn't laugh this time. It wasn't funny anymore.

The night air bit into her bare skin as her clothes pooled around her ankles, and Claire hopped up to wrap her legs around his waist. Zacharias mouthed at her neck, sucking the skin and pressing kisses which felt far too reverent.

"Come on," she hissed, thumping a fist weakly against his back. "Stop pretending."

Zacharias drew back and stared down at her, sorrow etched on his perfect face, but he swallowed and reached between them.

He paused at her entrance, eyes flicking to hers.

"I take a potion from the witches," Claire muttered, cheeks burning. "It's okay."

Not that he could get her pregnant anyway, but he was right, they should be safe; they should be careful with each other since they were basically strangers. They were one-time lovers, and this meant nothing.

He pushed inside her with maddening tenderness, pausing to let her adjust to the stretch. And Claire was horrified to realize tears brimmed in her eyes, and she stared up at the stars and the ribbons of dancing magic to keep them from spilling down her cheeks.

She didn't offer to let him bite her again. And he didn't ask. He thrust inside her, slowly at first, then picked up a rhythm. And she moaned and pushed back, meeting each thrust with her own, the slick slide of him almost too good to bear.

"Come for me," he said in her ear, his voice husky and low. He reached between them to skate a thumb over her bundle of nerves, and she cried out, winding her arms tighter around his shoulders. He worked her higher and higher, her breath coming in pants, until her nerves sang from the roots of her hair to her frozen toes and she clenched around him inside her. He grunted, vibrating with tension beneath her arms, but he waited until the last shudder of pleasure wracked through her before he allowed himself to let go.

It was so intimate to feel the rush of him inside her. Claire screwed her eyes shut and vowed to forget the sensation.

They stayed pressed together against the wall for a long minute, Zacharias' face buried in her neck. Then, when Claire finally cleared her throat, he straightened up and set her down on wobbly legs.

"Thanks," she muttered as he tucked himself away, then dug a cotton handkerchief out of his back pocket and knelt to wipe her clean.

"I started carrying one after my doorman was attacked." Zacharias dabbed at her, achingly gentle. "He ruined my favorite sweater."

Claire snorted—she couldn't help it—and the grin he shot her punched a hole through her rib cage. She stood there in a daze as he dressed her again, fastening the straps of her overalls before tugging his sweater over his head and putting that on her too.

It wasn't warm inside. Of course it wasn't; he had no body heat. But it was another layer, and Claire burrowed gratefully into the wool.

"Thanks," she rasped again, feeling like the world's biggest idiot. Were one-night stands always this awkward? "I'll wash it and send it back to your building."

He nodded, mouth set, and it was like they'd never had a reprieve from the bitter tension between them. Claire sighed, suddenly feeling a thousand years old, and stumbled back to the doorway. He let her go, still and watchful in the shadows, as she stepped back into the warmth and set off in search of her friends.

There would be no disguising what she'd been up to, not with her wild hair and raw, pink lips. Never mind that she wore his sweater... Claire fiddled with the cuffs as she walked down the stairs.

No, there was no escaping this. Bree would have a field day.

Chapter Sixteen

*A*fter three days apart from Claire Ramsden, Zacharias had hoped he'd return to normal. He'd be back to his standard, surly self, with his tolerable job and his inexplicable friends. And over time, the rawness he felt in his chest whenever he thought of her—that would heal.

So far, his heart made a mockery of him. He pined after his artist like a damned puppy, jumping at every voice across the street or chirp of his phone, his chest soaring at the thought it might be her.

Of course it wasn't her. It never was. He'd royally screwed this up.

One thing that *did* ease over time was the prickling awareness that he was a sap. The first night away from her, he'd roared in the privacy of his ruined apartment, barely containing the urge to destroy it all over again. But as the hours passed and his temper subsided, he came around to the situation with wry acceptance.

He was a wreck. A love-struck teenager, two hundred years

after it might have been cute. Zacharias waved goodbye to his self-respect and leaned into his new pathetic persona.

The evening was warm when he stepped out of his lobby, the day's heat still rising from the baked sidewalk. The sky was tinged pink and the stars glittered. A full moon shone over the rooftops, cratered and swollen.

Zacharias dug his hands into his pockets and set off down the street. He whistled as he walked, his footsteps light. Yes; wearing this tragedy suited him. It was like discovering a favorite old coat in the back of his closet and finding it still fit.

The deli was near the Main Street, almost exactly halfway between Claire's bungalow and the radio station. She'd seen it and thought of him, Zacharias mused, hopping up the two stone steps. The glass windows sparkled, the desert dust wiped away daily, and two bunches of red and green dried chilies hung on hooks on either side of the door frame. The shop display held cooked meat cutlets, bowls of stuffed olives, and wheels of exotic cheeses, but it was the bank of refrigerators behind the counter which drew his eye.

Blood. Delicious, organic blood, free from chemicals and preservatives. Harvested from happy, unstressed humans who were paid handsomely for their donations. The blood in those glass bottles were the work of the world's most pretentious vampires.

"One, please," he told the stocky man behind the counter, his barrel chest wrapped in a pristine white apron. Zacharias jerked his chin towards the row of blood bottles, just in case his fangs and chalky complexion weren't enough of a clue.

The man grunted and squeezed around in the narrow space, a waft of frosty, coppery air gusting across the deli when he opened the fridge door. Zacharias sucked in a deep breath and held it, smiling politely when the man turned back and placed the bottle on the counter.

"Thank you." He dropped the exact change in the man's palm and forced himself to take the bottle normally, without snatching. Zacharias congratulated himself silently as he exited the shop on a perfectly sane-sounding exchange.

"Oh!" The woman bounced off his chest, her platinum blonde hair flying over her face. Yelena, the troublesome podcaster, blinked up at him in shock, an iced coffee loaded with whipped cream in one hand and an iced doughnut in the other. Her gaze dropped to the smear of whipped cream on his shirt, and her cheeks pinked.

"Oh, gods. I'm so sorry." She moved to juggle her snacks into one manicured hand, her napkin flailing in the breeze. Zacharias held up a palm and dug out his handkerchief.

They were marvelous inventions. Now that he'd started carrying one, he couldn't understand why they'd gone out of fashion. He'd started a collection of white cotton squares, some embroidered with tiny bats and crescent moons.

"I've got it," he rumbled, dabbing at his own chest. For some reason, he didn't want Yelena to touch him. He was not exactly open to petting in general, and since the first moment he'd touched Claire, he might as well have built a force field around him. One crackling with electricity, and a red neon sign that proclaimed, "Claire Ramsden ONLY."

Yelena sighed and gave him a rueful smile. She waved her doughnut at him.

"You've caught me at a low moment."

Now *that* he could understand. Zacharias nodded, tucking his handkerchief away. The cap on his bottle screwed off easily, and he took a sip of the world's best blood.

Best from a bottle, anyway. There was nothing like straight from the source. But this would be it for Zacharias from now on—the thought of biting any person skin-to-skin who wasn't Claire was repellent.

"You and me both," he admitted after he swallowed, surprising them both. Every time Otis or Angie had urged him to talk over the last few days, he'd brushed them off with a snide remark. Apparently Zacharias was more in need of a confidant than he thought.

That was how he found himself sat on a bench in the Boiling River town square with a dejected podcaster at his side. They sipped their drinks in silence, both frowning at the empty air in front of them, as Yelena kicked her stilettos against the paving stones. Across the square, a flash of movement caught Zacharias' eye, and he waved at the shadow hunched on the roof of Hex Mex.

Gregor the gargoyle flipped him off, the gesture clear even across the square.

"It's work," Yelena blurted, jabbing her straw at her iced coffee. Only crumbs and a rumpled napkin remained of her doughnut. "I'm being called away from Boiling River. They want me on a new assignment."

"Okay..." Zacharias frowned at the rim of his bottle. Was he supposed to know what to say to that? "And this upsets you because...?"

"Because I want to stay!" Yelena tossed up her hands. "I hated it here at first, I thought we should raze the whole town, but the longer I stayed, the longer I felt sure that this is the place for me." Her eyes flicked shyly at Zacharias. "There are such... interesting people here."

Ah. This was awkward. Apparently even in his most pathetic

of states, Zacharias held humans under his sway. Perhaps Claire had been onto something when she marched into the radio station and accused him of using his glamor.

Was he using it now? Was he unknowingly trapping this poor woman? Zacharias shifted uneasily on the bench, putting a few more inches between them.

"Perhaps you'll feel the same way about your next destination. You won't know until you go there."

After all, what else had kept Zacharias moving from city to mountains and back? He'd been wholly transient before stumbling upon Boiling River. Upon Claire. Now, he knew right down to his marrow, he'd never leave this valley. Not while Claire was near; not with the memories of her so bright and clear.

"I don't want to try somewhere else." Yelena tore her napkin into vicious shreds. "I'm a woman who knows what she wants, Zacharias, and I've found that here. In Boiling River." She took a deep breath, her narrow shoulders rising around her ears. When she let it out in a gust, they dropped, and she turned her piercing blue eyes on him. "With you."

"I'm afraid you're mistaken," Zacharias told her, as gently as he could manage. Mostly, he wanted to get up and stride away. The moment Yelena began sliding him flirtatious glances, their sitting together had felt wrong. A betrayal of Claire somehow. He wanted no part of it. And some of that irritation must have bled through, because Yelena's expression hardened.

"Too human for you, Zacharias?"

He couldn't help the surprised laugh which burst out of his mouth. Yelena scowled, her sharp features fierce, and he choked his amusement back.

"Hardly. I'm spoken for, that's all."

134

"By a human woman?" Yelena frowned at him, eyes canny. Zacharias shrugged.

"It's irrelevant." *And private.* "I'm not interested in any others." Yelena's face crumpled, and Zacharias ground his fangs. Gods-damn it, he was trying here, trying to be patient and understanding and everything Claire would admire. But this whole conversation was utterly tedious, and he held about as much interest in this random woman's feelings as he did in Gregor's.

"Good night, Yelena." Zacharias pushed to his feet and paused before patting her shoulder. "Perhaps you'll have better luck on your next assignment."

She was so small on the bench, her frame birdlike, but the look she gave him made him jerk back instinctively.

"Fingers crossed," she hissed, voice heavy with sarcasm, and Zacharias nodded and turned on his heel. He strode briskly across the square, eager to put several blocks between himself and the bitter podcaster.

She could huff and snipe as much as she liked. It made no difference.

She wasn't Claire.

* * *

"You look like you just got back from a three-week bender to Hell."

Zacharias spun in his office chair and glared at the werewolf in his doorway. Yes, he was behind on his personal grooming these days, and yes, his interaction with Yelena had aged him about fifty years.

But to point it out? To kick him when he was down?

It was poor form.

"Thank you for that. I had no idea you were so concerned with my well being."

Otis grinned and crossed his arms.

"Can't escape it now, York. All pack members get the same treatment."

"I'm not a dog."

"And I'm not a bat, but somehow, we'll make it work."

"Oh, are you two dating?" Angie edged around the werewolf's bulk, her brown eyes wide with excitement. "I've always thought that would be cute."

Otis tipped back his head and roared with laughter as Zacharias scowled at the cupid. She ignored him, crossing to her desk and balancing a coffee cup and a spiral notebook on top of her closed laptop. The lid was covered with heart-shaped stickers and one especially ugly baby cherub.

"You truly are the worst cupid in existence."

Angie hummed. "Someone has to be."

While Angie unwound an impossibly long purple scarf, Zacharias returned his glare to Otis, where it belonged.

"I'm fine."

"You don't seem fine."

"I'm perfectly well."

"You don't seem perfectly—"

"Of course I'm not," Zacharias snapped. "I'm in love with a woman who hates my guts, and I'm being stalked by a psychotic fan. I live in arse-end-of-nowhere Boiling River, and I work with you clowns!"

He broke off, chest heaving, already regretting his outburst. It wasn't fair to lash out at Angie and Otis—besides their teasing, they'd only ever been good to him. But neither of them rankled at his harsh words. Otis' smirk widened, like he was watching a favorite TV show, and Angie hummed again but settled at her desk to stroke her plant.

"If you love her, what's the problem?" She ran a fingertip down the edge of a leaf, and the ticklish plant trembled.. "Go tell her how you feel."

"It's not that simple." Zacharias dug the heels of his palms into his eye sockets. How to explain this in a way they'd understand? How to convey the heartless way he'd frozen Claire out; her utter dismissal of him? Even after they'd joined on the roof, she'd been distant. Unreachable. He might as well have thrown himself on the mercy of an iceberg.

Otis snorted. "Yeah, it is. Suck it up. You've got your whole afterlife to be an idiot, York. Go talk to your girl."

Talk to her. Talk… to Claire.

He could tell her how he felt, he supposed. Bare his heart and soul, though his throat closed tight enough to make him wheeze at the very thought. He could kneel at her feet and beg her to give him one more try.

"Finish your shift, though." Otis winked. "You've had enough days off."

Zacharias huffed a laugh and settled back in his chair. Yes. A few hours' preparation would do no harm. He could write a pretty speech for Claire, duck home and tidy his appearance, then dash across Boiling River and win his lady back.

"Alright." Zacharias nudged Angie's chair with his boot. "But I'll need you on standby."

The smile she shot him was so full of warmth, it was how Zacharias imagined the rays of desert sun must feel.

"We always are, idiot. Like Otis said—you're one of the pack."

Chapter Seventeen

*C*laire barely noticed Bree thump a coffee down next to her sketchbook.

"Thanks," she called, a moment too late, but Bree waved her off from the register.

"It's decaf." Bree's eyebrow raised in challenge. "I'm cutting you off."

Claire poked her tongue out, then gathered the mug into her palms and took a sip. *Coffee.* Was there a better cure out there? Sure, her heart still ached in her chest, but her headache was long gone and her knee jiggled on her stool. The buzz from the Silver Bullet crowd washed over her—the clink of pool balls, the bursts of laughter, the hum of conversation—and Claire sipped her milky coffee and observed her work so far.

It was... good. Depressingly good. Not because she wanted to be a hack, obviously, but because it was a sketch of a certain vampire. His dark eyes burned with intensity as they stared at her from the page, exactly the way she remembered.

Gods. Bree's whole screw-him-out-of-your-system idea was

a total bust.

Propping her chin on her hand, Claire dragged her lump of charcoal across Zacharias' cheek. She shaded him slowly. Carefully. Like she might hurt him somehow if she pressed too hard or rushed it along.

Pathetic, really. Thank the gods he couldn't see her like this.

"Is this seat taken?"

Claire glanced up to find a woman in a pink blazer, black pants, and stilettos smiling at her brightly. She was petite, with silvery blonde hair tied back in elaborate braids.

"Sure," Claire said doubtfully. That blazer would not take well to charcoal. But the woman slid onto the stool beside her, rummaging in her patent leather bag. One by one, she placed a notebook, a fluffy pen, and a voice recorder on the stained wood of the bar.

Claire opened her mouth to ask, then shut it again. You know what? She didn't care.

"He's very handsome." The woman peered over Claire's shoulder as she sketched, her flowery perfume making Claire's nose itch. "Is he your boyfriend?"

Claire spluttered, fighting the urge to wave her hand under her nose.

"No." Jeez, did she have to sound so tragic about it? "He's just a model."

The woman hummed, like she'd eat Zacharias off a spoon if she had the chance. Claire couldn't really blame her, but a primal part of her still snarled in the back of her mind. Zacharias was *hers,* or at least... he had been.

Gods. Let him not have moved on already. It was such a depressing thought, when she was here, sketching him from memory like she could summon him through the page.

"I'm Yelena." The hand thrust under Claire's nose had jewel-tipped nails. "I'm interviewing Boiling River residents for a podcast."

"Sounds fun," Claire said flatly, turning back to her work. What was it about her that seemed so damn approachable? On buses, in the dentist's office, in the back of cabs—it was always the same. People saw her freckled cheeks and wanted to chat.

She could use some of Zacharias' brooding disdain. She frowned at her sketchpad, trying to mimic his scowl.

"Would you mind...?" The woman—Yelena—nudged her recorder closer on the bar, the light already green. Claire sighed, rubbing the bridge of her nose, remembering too late it would leave a charcoal smear.

"I'm human. If you want a supernatural interview, try the harpy in the corner. Or one of the demons playing pool."

"I know you're human." Yelena's eyes gleamed. "I want another perspective."

Claire chewed on her bottom lip. A reporter in Boiling River who gave a shit about humans? Who wanted to know more than the crap in the guidebooks? It was more than the town council bothered with. Claire drummed her fingers on the bar, glancing at Zacharias' stupid, perfect face, then tossed her charcoal onto the page and grabbed her coffee.

"Sure, why not? But let's move to a table. I'm about to fuse with this stool."

Claire's spine popped as she slid onto the bar floor, twisting from side to side and rolling her neck. She really needed to move more, to not get so wrapped up in her work, but she couldn't help it. The time she spent drawing or painting... it was like she got sucked into a pocket of time.

A metaphorical one. Not the time pocket next to the town

square bike racks.

"Perfect, thank you so much," Yelena gushed, leading the way across the bar. Her hips swung as she walked, her balance flawless on those sky-high heels, and Claire felt like some kind of ape, lumbering behind in her overalls, paint-splattered hair and sneakers.

Whatever. It wasn't like she had anyone to impress.

"So," Yelena breathed, fluttering her hands over her notebook and recorder as they smiled awkwardly at each other across the table. They'd found a quiet spot in a corner, away from the worst of the crowds, the sounds of the bar strangely distant. "How long have you lived in Boiling River?"

"Um," Claire said. She was not a born speaker. "My whole life. So twenty-four years?"

"How magical." Yelena flipped her notebook open and scribbled a note in looping cursive. "And how would you describe supernatural-human relations in the town?"

Claire shifted on her chair. She'd figured Yelena would ask about slice-of-life stuff. Human interest crap. Not local politics. "Fine," Claire hedged. "We're all just people, you know?"

It seemed petty to bring up the werewolves and her trash cans.

"And the man you were drawing," Yelena continued, like she hadn't even heard her. "This local model. Is he human too?"

"Uh…" Claire cast around for someone she recognized nearby, someone to save her from this mess she'd gotten herself into. She couldn't talk about Zacharias to a podcaster. The woman would figure out who he was in three seconds flat, and then Claire would have to listen to her go on and on about the famous vampire. About his husky, delicious voice and his legions of drooling fans.

No, thanks. Claire would rather jab herself in the eye with her charcoal.

"I'm not sure." She forced a smile for Yelena. "We didn't speak much. And you can't always tell."

"You don't speak with your models? But you were drawing him from memory. That seems terribly intimate." The podcaster leaned across the table, her wooden chair squeaking. "I don't think you're being honest with me, Claire."

"How do you…" Claire gripped the edge of the table with clammy palms. She hadn't given her name. She blinked down at the green light of the recorder, but its edges were fuzzy, blurring and splitting into two dots.

"What…" Claire's mouth wasn't working. Her tongue felt heavy, thick and slow in her mouth. She shook her head as Yelena helped her out of her chair, her feet walking obediently towards the bar door even as her brain screamed at them to stop. Claire opened her mouth to call out, but she couldn't even squeak—

Shadows crowded the edge of her vision. The cool night air prickled over Claire's cheeks as they stepped out onto Main Street, and Yelena's grip on her arm was tight enough to bruise.

"That's it," was the last thing Claire heard. The voice was muffled. "There's a good girl, Claire. Don't worry. We'll make this quick."

* * *

A stone sliced into Claire's cheekbone, jolting her awake. Dirt filled her mouth and nose—she was face-down, being dragged across the ground. Claire blinked hard, her vision blurry, and stifled a moan as a rattlesnake hissed near her ear.

Thump. Scrape. Thump. Scrape. Someone was dragging her across the desert, out into the wastes of the valley. Her fingertips scrabbled uselessly at the dirt, but she was weak and muddled, her brain scrambled in her skull.

What... how?

A headache was building behind her right eye, pulsing brighter and sharper until she had to screw that eye shut. Claire turned her head and blinked up with her left eye instead, the stars overhead bleeding into wobbly lines.

"Gods, you're heavy."

The voice came from her feet. From the death grip on her ankles. Claire tried to look down her own body, but her headache seared in response and she settled her cheek back against the dirt.

"Don't know..." There was a grunt. "What..." A muffled curse. "He sees in you."

Claire knew that voice. The tickle of recognition started in the back of her head and shivered down her spine. The reporter from the bar: Helena? No, Yelena. That petite woman in the impractical heels was dragging Claire through the desert.

If she wasn't so freaking angry, Claire would be impressed.

The desert was hard to navigate at the best of times, but with one cheek smushed in the dirt, it was even harder. Claire let her body relax, becoming as heavy as possible and narrowing her eye to a slit as she scanned her surroundings. Let Yelena think she was passed out again. Let her puff and sweat and drag Claire another ten meters. Claire needed to know where she was.

There was a cactus that looked kind of familiar, its arms raised in salute to the stars. And there were clusters of boulders, caked in dust and cratered like the moon overhead. On the edge of hearing, boiling water simmered.

The river, then. Well, there were far easier ways to kill someone, but maybe Yelena didn't have the stomach for them. Maybe she wanted it to look like an accident, or didn't want to get her blazer bloody.

Who knew? The woman was clearly out of her mind. Even now, after dragging Claire's lifeless body for what must have been an age, she was ranting and raving under her breath, carrying a full conversation with herself. Claire caught Zacharias' name a few times, and her stomach sank.

His crazy fan. She had to warn him.

Claire wriggled her fingers experimentally. Better. It was getting better. Her vision was clearing through the narrowed slit of her eye, and though her head was pounding worse than a girls' night hangover, her thoughts were untangling themselves.

This psycho. She'd drugged Claire somehow; dragged her like a sack of potatoes across the desert, past snakes and scorpion nests. She'd wrecked Zacharias' office, and then his apartment, and driven the two of them apart. And now she wanted to toss Claire in the river? In the Boiling River, that Claire grew up next to, and flicked pennies into for wishes, and skipped pebbles across its steaming surface?

Gods-damned tourists.

For all Yelena's grunting and cursing, she was strong enough to drag Claire this far. But she was so wrapped up in her own insane ramblings, she didn't see the kick coming until too late. Claire wrenched her ankle free and stomped out hard with her heel, catching Yelena square in the chest. The woman dropped her other foot and staggered back, wheezing and clutching the footprint on her t-shirt.

"What the hell?" Tears streaked down Yelena's face, glistening in the starlight. "That's so freaking rude."

"You're insane." Claire scrambled upright, planting her feet and squaring off with the tiny woman. The stars swam overhead, and for a moment Claire swayed before blinking hard and finding her balance. "You're out of your mind."

Yelena gave a great sniff, her lip wobbling as she tried in vain to brush the dirt off her t-shirt.

"This is Prada," she whispered. Then her eyes narrowed, and she glared up at Claire. "You'll pay for that."

As far as Claire could tell, she'd already done a lifetime's worth of penance. Her joints throbbed; her mouth tasted like dirt; and this headache was trying to split her skull in two.

"Try me." She wiped her nose on her arm. "I'd love to kick your ass."

It was bluster—Claire hadn't been in a fight since middle school—but there was truth to it, too. Yelena may be insane, but she was a grade A bitch, and Claire knew she'd hurt Zacharias next. Yes, he had supernatural strength and glamor and all that crap, but he was a gentleman. He'd give her the edge just to be fair.

Claire, though? She didn't care about fair. She wanted to get this freaking nightmare over with. So when Yelena roared and charged at her, arms outstretched, Claire braced herself and met her head on. It was almost too easy, grappling with the tiny woman and throwing her to the side. And maybe she was bloodthirsty, but Yelena's shriek at being tossed into a cactus filled Claire with savage joy.

"Oh, yeah." Claire rolled her head on her neck. "I should do this more often."

Crimson spread over the horizon line, staining the sky blood red. And Claire beat the podcaster into the dirt, grinning like a maniac when the smaller woman got in a good few shots.

"Get. Off." Yelena grunted as Claire tackled her waist, slinging her over her shoulder. She staggered under the weight, especially as the little psycho writhed and kicked, but Claire had no intentions of carrying her all the way back across the desert. No; there was a hole near here, penned in by steep walls on all sides. That should hold Yelena until the Boiling River cops arrived.

"This is generous," Claire panted, squinting at the shadowed landscape. She stumbled along the bank, searching for the hole, the river steam clinging damp to her cheeks. "You're lucky I don't toss you in the river."

A searing pain tore through her left calf, burning hot in her flesh. Claire yelled, her leg buckling, and dropped to one knee. Yelena tumbled off her shoulder and scrambled into a crouch, a bloody shard of stone clutched in one fist.

"I didn't want to do that," Yelena said, her bright eyes showing her lie. Her chest heaved, her dainty collar bone thrusting against her t-shirt. "You made me."

Claire pressed a hand to her calf, and when she brought it away, her palm was sticky and dark. Fluid soaked her overalls, spreading through the denim and making it cling to her skin.

Bile rose in her throat, and she choked it back. She could freak out later. When Yelena wasn't straightening up, mouth firm with resolve as she adjusted her grip on the stone shard. Claire raised her palms and braced as Yelena lunged, swiping the stone.

The podcaster's yell cut off as she jerked into the air, held by the scruff of her neck by a pale hand. Zacharias looked at her, mouth turned down with disdain, then tossed her into a cactus like a napkin into the trash.

Yelena wailed, sprawled over the spines, and sobbed as she kicked her way free.

"You hurt me." Her legs wobbled as she stood on the river's edge. "This will never work if you hurt me." She scrubbed at the red lines on her arms, and the vampire's nostrils flared.

Claire watched from the dirt as Yelena looked up, her eyes brimming with tears. And she held her breath as the tiny woman took a step toward Zacharias, one hand outstretched.

"We can fix this," the podcaster breathed, then Claire yelled as the tiny woman lunged with the stone. It arced through the air, swiping across Zacharias' chest, tearing his shirt but barely grazing the skin beneath. He knocked her hand away, annoyed, like an older cat batting away a kitten, and she stumbled back.

"I'm sorry," she hiccoughed, "I didn't mean it—"

Yelena broke off as her stiletto heel snapped. She lurched to one side, arms flailing, her mouth dropping open as she stepped off the riverbank onto thin air. Zacharias reached for her, and Claire's mouth started to form a shout, but the podcaster was already falling towards the milky, churning river.

Her scream rent the desert, then cut off abruptly. Silence hung, then crickets began to chirp.

"That was easy." Zacharias eyed the simmering water. "The trash took itself out."

Maybe it was heartless, but Claire couldn't bring herself to care either.

"You're here." Claire squeezed the wound on her calf tighter as Zacharias dropped to his knees beside her. Even in the dawn gloom, she could see his nostrils flare and his jaw clench.

Dawn.

The sunrise.

"Of course I'm here," Zacharias grunted. "Don't be dramatic."

He glanced down, surprised, as Claire clutched his sleeve and shook him.

"Zacharias. The sun."

There were minutes left. Mere moments until the sun burst into the paling sky. Claire cast around for shade, for somewhere for him to hide, but this was the desert. They were miles from town, from the nearest roofs and curtains, and she'd only just got Zacharias back and now she'd have to watch him turn to ash—

"No," Claire croaked, burying her face in his shoulder. He shifted, winding his arms around her and gathering her against his chest. His hand was steady as it rubbed her back.

"It doesn't matter," he told her gently. "I'd always choose this, Claire. I'd choose you."

She drew back, an ache throbbing in her chest. Her heart crumpled in on itself. And he dipped his head, the dirt in her mouth be damned, and kissed her as the sun rose over the mountains.

Chapter Eighteen

∽◦◦◦◦∾

The horn blared through the still desert air, shocking Zacharias away from Claire. He gripped her shoulders, head jerking as he searched the area and frowned at the trail of dust floating towards the purple sky. A van bounced across the desert, rocking on its tires and launching into the air before landing with a crash. It lurched towards them, tires spinning and metal screaming, and Zacharias pulled Claire to her feet as he recognized the loud-hailer wobbling on the roof rack.

"Get over here, you dumbass!" Otis' voice echoed across the field of boulders, tinny and metallic. Zacharias lunged forward a step, then paused, glancing back at Claire. She was ashen with pain, swaying and keeping all her weight on one foot.

She rolled her eyes and shoved his arm. "You really are a dumbass."

The mountains tinged pink as Zacharias raced across the dirt, leaping over a coiled rattlesnake and kicking up a trail of dust. Otis leaped out of the van, racing to the back and throwing the rear doors open. He squatted, waving Zacharias closer and yelling at him to hurry up. Angie's face pressed against the passenger window, her mouth a perfect 'O'.

Sunshine burst into the valley, sweeping down the mountain-side in a golden wave. Zacharias thought of coppery hair and paint-splattered overalls, and put on a final, desperate burst of speed. His skin began to sizzle just as he launched into the back of the van, the doors slamming shut behind him and plunging him into blissful, velvety darkness.

The sizzling stopped.

"Damn! That was close." Otis whooped outside, his voice fading as he walked away. Towards Claire, Zacharias hoped, to help her too, else he'd have to kill the man who just saved his afterlife. He scrambled up onto his knees, pressing his ear against the metal shell of the van, willing his pounding heart to quiet so he could listen.

Angie shifted in the front seat. Her voice was timid as she called through the cab wall.

"Are you okay back there?"

Was he okay? He'd just escaped being burned to ash by a fraction of a second, and now he couldn't see or hear Claire, couldn't tell if she was alright—

Zacharias thumped on the van wall in response. He couldn't bring himself to speak.

It took an age for Otis and Claire to reach the van, and Zacharias' gut churned the whole time. First and foremost, and gods, he hated himself for this—he was so damn thirsty. His throat clenched on nothing, cutting off his airways, and hunger clawed at his insides. Then was the fear, the mind numbing panic that took over him when he thought of Claire, of the sticky wound on her leg.

Yelena. His rabid fan. It was all his fault. He was the one she wanted really, and he'd led her to Claire. His artist nearly died because of him, all because of his foolishness.

She may never forgive him. Part of him hoped that she wouldn't; it was what he deserved.

Then there was the small matter of watching a woman die. Oddly enough, that part didn't bother Zacharias. He examined his feelings while he waited, teased them apart to look closer, but no. He wasn't even a little bit sorry.

"There you go." Otis' voice was muffled by the metal, but he could hear the werewolf helping a limping Claire into the cab. Her breathing was quick and ragged, her pain clear even from inside the van, and Zacharias clenched his jaw so hard his teeth ached. He lashed out, punching whatever was heaped beside him, and was rewarded with a shower of sweetener packets.

"Oi." Otis thumped on the cab wall, slamming the van door behind him. "You make a mess back there and next time you'll ride in the puppy cage."

Zacharias eyed the looming wire structure across the van. It was not an empty threat. He called to Claire through the metal.

"Ramsden? Are you alright?"

She huffed a laugh, the sound faint but glorious. If Zacharias could, he'd record that sound and set it as his ringtone. He'd play it on the radio for his shift: a constant loop until someone complained.

"Yeah." Her voice was thin, threaded with pain, but he could hear her smiling. "Your fans are nuts, by the way."

"They'd have to be," Zacharias murmured, pressing a palm against the cab wall, closing his eyes as she laughed again.

She was safe. Hurt, yes, but his Claire was a survivor. Zacharias rested his forehead against the cab wall and listened

151

to her breathing all the way back to town.

* * *

Otis drove them to the underground parking at Zacharias' apartment. The vampire burst out of the van as soon as Otis thumped on the metal, almost ripping the doors off their hinges.

"Careful, man!" Otis squatted, frowning at the twisted metal. "This van is precious."

"Sorry," Zacharias lied, already tugging the passenger door open. Angie winked, sliding out of the van and ducking out of the way. Claire sat bundled in the cab, a sweater tied around her calf. "Bad night?" he asked, far more casually than he felt.

She grinned, and his chest soared in answer. Claire shuffled across the seat, wincing in pain, and let him scoop her into his arms.

"I can walk, you know." She pressed the tip of her nose to his throat.

He scoffed. "I don't believe you can."

It hadn't occurred to Zacharias to fantasize about this: carrying Claire Ramsden bridal style over the threshold of his apartment. Given the choice, he'd rather she weren't cringing in pain, and they were much more alone.

Still, it felt right. The ache in his chest eased slightly.

"I'm keeping you here," he told her conversationally as he carried her across his apartment. With Otis and Angie's help, he'd cleared the worst of the wreckage, and he'd cobbled one sofa back together. He lay her there, tucking a throw over her lap and propping her wounded leg on a cushion. "You probably thought you were done being abducted. I'm sorry, Claire, but you were wrong."

She laughed, the sound cutting off with a gasp as she shifted in pain.

"It's not abduction if I'm willing."

"Is that so?" He traced a fingertip over her cheek. "I lose track of your puny, human laws." He couldn't keep his eyes off her—not her dust-caked skin, her chipped tooth, or her blood-crusted clothes. Her hair was tangled and clumped with dirt; her green eyes were pink and sore.

Zacharias had never seen a more perfect sight in his afterlife. Especially the sight of her *here*, on his sofa, in his home. His threat had been a joke, but part of him—the ancient, brutal part—yearned to make it come true.

He never wanted to let her go. He couldn't bear it.

"You've gone all monster-eyed." Claire poked his leg. Behind him, Angie and Otis both spoke into their phones; one to the police, and one to the hospital. When an ambulance left to drive the few blocks to his apartment, siren blaring, Zacharias heard it coming.

He knelt at her side, twirling a lock of her hair around his finger. "I *am* a monster."

"Only sometimes."

His mouth twisted. He never wanted to be monstrous to her.

"It's kind of sexy," Claire whispered, even though there was no way Otis' werewolf ears wouldn't hear. Zacharias didn't tell her so. He wanted her to keep talking, to keep looking at him like that. "Don't tell anyone I said that, though."

Across the room, Otis stifled a laugh. Zacharias cracked a rare smile. "I promise."

* * *

It was becoming a theme between him and Claire: chaotic nights followed by long, exhausted days. They got through it powered by coffee for Claire and blood for Zacharias, and by shooting each other shy smiles across the breadth of his apartment.

Otis hung around long enough to let the EMTs and the police officers in. Then he tucked Angie under his arm, saluted to Zacharias, and strolled chuckling into the elevator.

The questions were led by the leopard shifter Claire called Danny. Zacharias watched him with thinly veiled contempt, rubbing his thumb over the rim of his blood bottle, contemplating whether the officer would taste like cat. The man pulled up a chair and sat beside Claire, scribbling in his notebook as a recorder balanced precariously on his knee. Claire answered as best she could, even when the sting of the EMT's antiseptic on her wound made her hiss through her teeth.

Zacharias stepped forward, but Claire shot him a warning look and waved him off.

Fine. Zacharias leaned against his bookcase, chastened. He would watch from a distance. But the second the idiot officer overstepped or pushed too far, he would toss him by the ear from the apartment.

When it was his turn to speak to the officer, Zacharias answered each question with clipped responses and a stony expression. Yes, it had been suicide. No, he hadn't killed her. Yes, he was sure. Round and round the conversation went, Officer Daniel grilling him and trying to trip him up.

"Don't leave town," the leopard shifter told him at last, glowering as he tucked his notepad away.

Zacharias looked over his shoulder, straight into Claire's eyes, and said, "I don't plan to."

By the time they were finally alone, the clock on the wall showed it was gone midday. Claire's stomach growled from the sofa, and Zacharias launched upright and strode to his barely-used kitchen. It was decorative, mostly, apart from the refrigerator for his blood. An artistic flourish; a nod to once being human.

It could be so much more now, though. The thought of Claire coming here and eating food he made her… Zacharias made a mental note to order some cookbooks.

"It's alright," she called, her voice rough. "Zacharias. I'm not hungry."

"Liar," he said mildly, digging through his cupboards for something she could eat. "I can hear your stomach."

"Let's order, then." She didn't suggest going home. It pleased him more than he'd ever thought possible. Even trussed up and dirty on his sofa, leg wound bound but the rest of her still battered, she wanted to stay here. She trusted him to take care of her. "In a minute, though. We need to talk."

His good mood sank like a stone.

Of course she was angry. It was his fault she'd been mauled by a crazed fan, and even before that he'd been an utter ass. Zacharias closed the cupboard, lingering to take a steadying breath through his nose.

Claire sighed as he crossed to her with the air of a condemned man walking to the noose.

"Stop it." She tugged at his sleeve when he came within reach, pulling him down to squash on the sofa beside her. "Stop being so tragic."

Zacharias straightened his shoulders and forced a smile over his cheeks.

"Gods, no." Claire flapped a hand at him. "That's even worse."

There was nothing for it. Zacharias sat in silence, aiming for a blank expression while his heart crumbled to ash in his chest.

"I think I might love you." Claire's voice was hoarse. "I know it's way too soon, and you don't want this, but I need to say it." She swallowed hard—so brave, always so brave. "In the desert, when I thought I'd lost you—"

"Me too," Zacharias said quickly. She'd been vulnerable long enough. "I think I love you too. I wouldn't just have killed Yelena. I'd have burned the whole town—the whole *continent* to ash."

"Good thing it didn't come to that." Claire's lip wobbled when she smiled. "I wouldn't want that, by the way."

"Noted," Zacharias murmured, leaning down to bury his nose in her hair. He breathed in, sucking her scent into his lungs, the hint of basil and tangerine and turpentine still there under the dirt and blood. She was safe. She loved him. She was his.

He didn't deserve her, but he would spend the rest of his afterlife trying to earn her love. Starting with her current discomfort, and the tang of her arousal in the air. Zacharias flicked one of her overall straps open, sliding it off her shoulder, and moved straight to the next.

"You're getting good at that," Claire said breathlessly, shifting to give him better access. He smirked at her, peeling her overalls down to her waist then shimmying them over her hips. She reached for him—what, did she think he wanted sex while she was in pain? Zacharias rolled his eyes, tugging the blood-soaked denim over her ankles and tossing it with her sneakers to the floor.

"I need to shower." She plucked at his hair. "I probably smell like the dead."

"Should I take offense to that?" he mused aloud, pressing a

kiss against the inside of her knee. Goosebumps erupted over her bare thighs, and Zacharias hummed and stroked her skin with his palm. "Let me help," he murmured, his voice husky. "Let me make you feel good."

He wouldn't screw her, not when the jostling would risk pain or damage to her wound. But there was another natural painkiller available to Claire, gathering in beads at the tips of his fangs.

"Oh gods. Shit." Claire was rambling, eyes wide and pupils blown as he stroked her legs. "Okay. But don't blame me if I'm gross."

"You are literally incapable of being gross," he promised, pressing her legs apart. His fingers hooked in the waistband of her underwear, and she shivered beneath him. "You are a gourmet meal."

"Now *you're* being—" Claire cut off with a moan as Zacharias leaned forward and licked a stripe up her core. Her hands buried in his hair, gripping and tugging, and he slid a hand to the task too. He worked her in tandem, by hand and by tongue, and when she was quaking and mewling beneath him, he drifted his mouth to her inner thigh. Her blood rushed under her skin, staining it pink, the sound and scent of it calling to him like the moon to the wolves.

"Tell me if you want me to stop." She shook her head, eyes glassy, watching as he opened his mouth and bared his fangs. Her breath quickened as he lowered his head to her thigh, resting his teeth against her skin.

Zacharias paused, his undead heart thundering in his chest, but she didn't stop him. If anything, she squirmed more urgently against his hand.

When his fangs broke her skin, her blood filled his mouth,

rich and earthy and decadent. It was the best thing he'd ever tasted. All other blood would taste like mud after this, and Zacharias couldn't help but groan and clutch her leg closer. Her muscle was tense at first, shivering under her grip, but as his venom spread through her body, Claire relaxed and began to moan louder.

Yes. That was another pleasing side effect.

As her pain lessened, Zacharias forced himself to release Claire's leg, swiping his tongue over the skin to seal the puncture wounds. Then, glassy-eyed himself from the euphoria of her blood, he set himself back to his task. He toyed with her; he made her weep with frustration even as she dragged him closer. And finally, finally, he coaxed her to come, her orgasm thundering through her battered frame.

Claire slumped back against the sofa cushions. Her chest heaved beneath her t-shirt, and her hand shook as she reached out to smooth his hair. Zacharias leaned into the touch like a cat, shameless in his need for her affection.

"What shall we order?" Claire said at last.

Zacharias snorted. "This one's on you. I already ate."

As he wedged in beside her, scrolling through the open Boiling River restaurants on his phone, Zacharias couldn't help the smile stretching his cheeks.

It didn't seem possible. But she was here, and she wanted to stay.

Epilogue

Three Months Later

Claire wiped her palms on the front of her shorts, gazing up at the nursing home. At first glance, it blended in with the townhouses on either side, tucked away in a sleepy outskirt of Boiling River. Window boxes hung from sills, filled with succulents and flowering cacti, and the pale stone was buffed clean by the desert breeze.

"I'm not sure about this."

It hurt to admit, and it was probably worse for Zacharias to hear. But her dad had lost the love of his life to a vampire's charm. And even though his mind was part way gone, Claire wasn't sure how well the remaining parts of her father would take to her new boyfriend.

Boyfriend. It was such a frivolous word for a two-hundred-something year old vampire. A bloodthirsty predator; a creature of the night.

The monster in question took her hand and squeezed.

"We don't have to do this today. We can come back another time. Or never, if you prefer." Zacharias looked at the front of the building as he spoke, and if Claire hadn't been watching him closely, she might have missed the flicker of sorrow passing over his face.

He wanted to meet her father. To tie the two of them even closer together. But he wouldn't insist, wouldn't force her into anything, and she loved him for that.

"We're doing this." She squeezed his hand in return, and Zacharias shot her a faint smile. He wore the most formal outfit she'd seen him in yet: a dark blue button down shirt and black pants. He almost looked like the other fancy vampires. It was sweet that he'd dressed up to meet her dad, but she missed his black t-shirts and scuffed jeans. At least strands of his dark hair still curled around his face, escaped from their tie.

It was early evening, and the lights of the nursing home were still on, spilling squares of buttery warmth out into the shadowed street. Claire led the way up the front steps, knocking twice on the door and pushing it open with the casual confidence of someone who'd been here many times before. Inside, a television blared down the hall, and a dinner trolley squeaked as it was pushed along a lumpy rug to deliver cakes and hot chocolates to the residents.

"Claire-Bear!" Delilah, one of the nurses, called through an open doorway where she was rubbing lotion into a resident's legs. Delilah was a plump elderly woman almost old enough to check in. Almost everyone living in the Boiling River nursing home was ancient—literally in the case of some supernaturals—except for the unlucky few who'd fallen ill earlier in life.

It wasn't fair. It would never feel fair. Claire's stomach still churned with the injustice of it all.

"How is he?"

"Oh, fine." Delilah brushed her hands together, then heaved to her feet, pushing off the resident's armchair. "Very excited to meet your man." Delilah eyed Zacharias over Claire's shoulder with shameless appreciation. Claire suppressed a snort, especially when Zacharias stepped closer to her back.

"I'll protect you," she murmured as she led him along the hall.

"I'm going to need it." His fingers playing in her hair.

Claire's dad was in his usual spot: stood at an easel in the room with the biggest windows, frowning down at his work and flicking paint everywhere. The nurses put down newspapers to try and protect the floorboards, but Claire had already resigned herself to paying for their next re-decorations.

"Hi, Dad." Her father's head jerked up, and a smile like sunshine spread over his face. He was wan, old before his time, but his sparkling green eyes were creased with laughter lines, and his red hair was thick and bushy. "What are you working on?"

"Oh, nothing." He waved a hand, splattering globs of blue paints over the wall. "Nothing like the things you paint, Claire-Bear."

Claire's moderate success as a professional artist was a source of intense pride for her dad. He liked to brag that it was his raw talent, passed down and honed in his daughter. She couldn't tell whether he was teasing her when he said that or whether he meant it, but she didn't care either way.

It was true. All the good parts of her were thanks to him.

"Dad." Claire cleared her throat, reaching blindly behind her to grab Zacharias' shirt and jerk him forward. "There's someone I want you to meet. Um. Someone important."

Zacharias stepped around her fully, offering a hand to her father. They muttered greetings, and Claire held her breath as they shook hands and her dad's eyebrows shot up his forehead. The gears turned visibly in his head: cold skin, pale, handsome, his daughter gnawing her lip with nerves. And a flicker of hurt passed over his face before he dropped his hand.

"Got yourself a vamp, have you, Claire-Bear?" her dad asked quietly, his eyes fixed on the man beside her. He picked up a rag from his easel and wiped at a splatter of dried paint on his wrist.

She could see it all again: her mother's abandoned sewing machine. The closet still packed with her clothes. The grief etched over her dad's kind features.

"Zacharias." She said it with as much force as she could muster. "His name is Zacharias. And it's nothing like with Mom."

Zacharias rubbed a palm over the small of her back, and the motion grounded her. It would be okay. Dad would grow to love him as much as she did, and they would all laugh about this one day. Until then…

"Good to meet you, son." Her dad nodded at the vampire more than twice his age. He pointed his paintbrush at Zacharias, but a smile tugged at his mouth. "Now you be good to her, or I'll sharpen up my stakes."

It was such a ridiculous, empty threat, and Claire's heart swelled to hear Zacharias chuckle.

"Yes, sir," he murmured, so patient and polite, and Claire closed her eyes for a moment. She focused on the tang of paint and turpentine; the cool breeze drifting through the open window; the hum of voices around them. She focused on the solid body at her side, a constant wall of support, and the twinkle in her dad's green eyes as he teased Zacharias.

It was more than she could have hoped for. More than she'd dreamed.

She took Zacharias' cool hand and squeezed.

* * *

"We're going to be late." She tugged Zacharias across the town square, towards the turning for the Silver Bullet. "If we're not careful, Bree and Otis will be there on their own, and then all that's left will be a huge, smoking crater."

"My money's on Bree," came the smoky voice behind her. Zacharias let her pull him along but refused to speed up, shooting her a smirk when she glared over her shoulder.

"Are you trying to be a pain in the ass?"

"No." He tugged her to a stop in the center of the square. "I simply have different priorities." He nodded over her shoulder and Claire spun around, blinking up at the roof of Hex Mex. She jumped when Zacharias leaned forward to murmur in her ear, his lips brushing her earlobe. "Let's evict Gregor for ten minutes. For old times' sake."

Claire snorted, even as her breath came faster. He knew he had this effect on her, the damn vampire, he knew he made her core clench and her skin flush hot and pink.

"Gregor already hates us." Someone had to be the voice of reason.

"Then who cares?" Zacharias said smoothly. "The damage is done."

Claire bit her lip, her mind flashing back to their last visit to the Hex Mex roof. To the way he'd stripped her and pushed her up against the brick wall, to the way he drove inside her—

"Fine." She was breathless and weak, but she couldn't bring herself to care. When she turned back around, Zacharias' eyes were bright with triumph. "But make it quick."

"So romantic," he teased, pulling her across the square to Hex Mex. The sidewalk already thronged with tourists, clad in alien-spotter t-shirts and wearing headbands with fake horns.

"Don't even think about it!" Gregor called from the roof, his voice echoing and distant, but Zacharias ignored him, pushing open the club's front door as the gargoyle cursed from above.

Claire would make it up to him. Send a gift basket or something. Or offer to paint him a mural on his roof. And one day, when the gargoyle found someone, he could come and kick them out of Claire's bungalow. Fair was fair, Claire thought as they jogged up the stairs, and there was a decent chance Gregor would find love.

After all, what kind of obstacle was a body made of stone?

Anything could happen in Boiling River.

THE END

Something is haunting Olivia...

Want to know what's bothering the town librarian?

Check out this free short story about one of Boiling River's most mysterious residents: https://BookHip.com/PKKRSH

Love Otis and Bree?

Epilogue

Check out the world's most disastrous pairing in Howl FM.

& If you liked this story, please consider leaving a review!

Teaser: Howl FM

⚜

Howl FM, the second book in the Supernatural Airwaves series comes out in January 2021. Read on for a sneak preview...

*　*　*

The front door was shattered. It hung crooked on its hinges, its wood splintered and warped, the paint gouged away in huge strips. Bree Mendez stared from the sidewalk, clenching her backpack strap in one hand and her bike helmet in the other. Cars rumbled along the street behind her, the sleepy morning traffic oblivious to the wreckage on the side of the road.

"Shit."

She nudged a shard of glass with the toe of her boot. It crackled across the paving stone. Broken glass littered the sidewalk, glittering in the crisp morning light, and the front of the Silver Bullet bar loomed in front of her, its windows punched in like a boxer's teeth.

"Shit," Bree said again. It bore repeating.

If this was a horror movie—one of the ones she watched most weekends, crammed on her sofa with the girls—she'd push the door open and walk inside. It'd be dark, too, and the door would creak on its hinges, and she'd call out for intruders as she walked blindly into the shadowed bar.

Screw that. Even first thing in the morning, Bree wasn't that dumb. She dug out her phone and called 911.

Boiling River may have been a small town, but the emergency lines were kept busy. It was natural, when the town was home to one of the biggest populations of supernatural creatures in the country.

Tempers ran high in the heat. Instincts were not always tamed. Accidents happened. And the tourists freaking loved that shit, poring over news articles and hoping for a mauling.

Bree was not a tourist. She just wanted to start her shift.

"Yeah, hi." The phone operator barked out questions as Bree relayed the scene. Yes, she worked here. No, she hadn't gone inside. No, she had no idea what happened. She eyed the building as they talked, wincing at the lines gouged into the front door and the shadows of wrecked furniture inside.

"Are valuables kept in the bar overnight?" The operator said everything in the same loud, clipped tone, like a drill sergeant giving commands. Bree grit her teeth, tamping down the urge to snipe back. She was reporting a crime, not screwing around.

"No." Besides cash, the only things worth a dime in the Silver Bullet were the retro jukebox and the speaker system. "Charlton takes the lock box home with him every night."

"That's not safe." Triumph rang down the phone line, like he'd caught Bree being careless. She rolled her eyes up at the gutters. As if she held any sway over her cranky old boss.

"He also takes a loaded shotgun."

The operator spluttered. "That's not safe either!"

… Alright. Bree was not a morning person, and this guy had

167

reached the end of her rope. She squeezed the phone in her hand, forcing cheeriness into her voice as she kicked at the glass again.

"Cool, well, you should probably send someone over! Thanks for your help."

"Wait, hang on miss—"

She jabbed the screen with her thumb. Life was too damn short.

The morning sun shone hot on the back of her neck, and Bree rolled her head in a circle. It was stiff, the muscles sore from falling asleep on her sofa watching true crime documentaries at 3am. When she'd woken up this morning, she'd still been wearing last night's work t-shirt, the smell of stale beer wafting up from the fabric.

Gods, she needed a reset.

Bree clicked her tongue. This was Boiling River. The cops could be three minutes or three hours. Glass crunched under her boots as she strode to the bar's outer wall, tossing her backpack and bike helmet down in a heap. Then Bree turned, leaned her back against the brick, and tipped her face up to the sun.

An aching back. An overslept alarm. A half-destroyed bar. It was just another day in Boiling River, the desert town that had tethered her since birth.

Bree gusted out a heavy breath, closed her eyes, and wished for something interesting to happen.

* * *

There were lots of reasons a building might get wrecked in Boiling River.

Drunken tourists.

A sinkhole.

The wrath of a local god.

"Werewolves," Bree's boss Charlton declared as soon as he arrived. He scowled at the front of his ruined bar, hands shoved deep in the pockets of his leather vest, his shoulders bunched by his ears. He was a grizzly, grumbling ex-biker who'd settled in the valley when his hog broke down in Boiling River back in the eighties. He told Bree once the cost of fixing his prized bike or buying a tumbledown cottage out here were about the same.

Bree believed it. A couple years back, she'd saved up enough to take off and backpack around the world for six months. She'd thought she had enough for a year, but turns out Boiling River was dirt cheap compared to the big, wide world.

Apparently most people didn't want to live in the ass-crack of nowhere with a bunch of fairy tale monsters.

"Maybe." Bree scuffed her boot on the sidewalk. It was always supernatural creatures who got blamed for the slightest crime. And though those claw marks on the door were pretty damning, she wasn't about to throw around accusations without proof. "Danny will tell us more."

Charlton snorted, his salt and pepper mustache fluttering. "That boy? He's only just outta diapers."

Danny was two years older than Bree. She said nothing.

Once upon a time, Bree was known around town as a firecracker—quick to anger, with a temper flashing hot. These days, though, she was more listless than lively. Her spark had gone out. She still went through the motions, tossing back shots behind the bar and chasing out sloppy drinkers with a pool cue, but her heart wasn't in it.

169

She shrugged. "He's gone through all the training. Danny's a good cop." She spoke to the single cloud drifting across the desert sky, like a cotton ball caught in a stream.

Charlton grumbled something under his breath. It must have been bad for him to mumble. He was a grouchy old fool, and vicious when he wanted to be, but Bree knew him better than anyone. He gave her this job when she dropped out of college and came back to Boiling River. And when her family moved to the west coast without her, he rented Bree her shitbox apartment at a fair rate.

After all these years, Charlton was family. Just… the kind of family that started fights at Thanksgiving.

The police car pulled up to the curb, the windows wound down and the radio humming. The police handset crackled over the music, calling out codes and street locations.

"Hey, Danny," Bree called as the leopard shifter killed the engine. He unfolded himself from the car, all graceful long limbs. "You draw the short straw?"

"Yes, ma'am." Danny was always so damn formal on duty. He'd been the same way when Claire was attacked by her vamp boyfriend's stalker a few months back. All *Miss Ramsden* and *a moment of your time*—like they hadn't all known him as a teenager sneaking bottles away to party in the valley. "We got your call about a break in." He leveled her a look. "You could have stayed on the line."

Bree gave a sharp smile. "No, I couldn't."

"It's for your safety."

"And look! I survived."

They could have gone on for a while, bickering like old friends, but Charlton cleared his throat then spat on the sidewalk. He stepped up to Danny, barrel chest straining his vest, white hairs curling over the zipper.

"This is the wolves' doing. See those claw marks?"

Danny glanced over his shoulder and nodded once, short and sharp.

"I see them. Lots of creatures round here with claws." He raised an eyebrow at the old biker, as if to remind him that *he* was one of them.

"It's the wolves," Charlton repeated, stubborn. "They're always raising Hell in my bar. Breaking glasses and knocking down stools." Danny whipped out a pad, scribbling a note and waving for Charlton to keep talking. Bree rolled her eyes and pushed away from the wall, strolling closer to the front door as they talked. Get Charlton started on one of his rants and you'd have three more gray hairs by the time it ended.

There were four claw marks total. Gouged deep into the wood, they stretched from her head height down to her waist. Bree sucked on her teeth, raising a hand and mimicking the shape of the slash.

"Don't touch that," Danny called out, voice curt. What was it with lawmen barking at her today? "That's evidence."

"I'm not an idiot," she called back without turning around. "Can I touch the air, Officer Danny? Or is that evidence too?"

Charlton guffawed behind her, and that told her to ease off. If her boss found her funny, she was usually being an ass. Bree stepped away from the door, palms held up, then stuffed her hands in her pockets. She could play nice.

Craning her neck, Bree peered through the shattered windows. The inside looked even worse than the front door—floorboards pried up; the pool table knocked on its side. Broken glass glittered from the floor.

No way were they opening up today. Not even if they could

start cleaning up right now. Bree was down a shift, and with it, in trouble with her bank. Again.

"You need me here?" she called, cutting over Danny. If she could go now, maybe she could swing a shift at Hex Mex…

"Afraid so." Danny really did look sorry, his brown eyes knowing. Like he could see the tiny numbers flashing through her brain, see the panic brewing in her gut. It made her itch. "I'll need to take a statement, and then it would be good to have you here for the walk through. To see if anything's out of place."

Bree scoffed. "The whole damn bar's out of place." But she stomped back to the wall and leaned there again.

With her head tipped back and her eyes closed, Charlton's rant faded to a low hum. Passing traffic rumbled along the street, the vibrations buzzing through the sidewalk, and the rays of sunshine soaked into her skin. It was almost nice, if she let herself forget why she was here. Almost restful…

"Good morning, sunshine." A deep voice jerked Bree awake. She leaped forward, staggering away from the wall where she'd been dozing. Danny and Charlton were still huddled together talking, further down the sidewalk now, and the lone cloud was gone from the sky.

"Never took you for a napper."

Gods damn it. She should have known. The second Charlton had said wolves, she should have known they'd call *him*.

Otis Pascale. The Boiling River alpha. And the bane of Bree's existence.

* * *

Otis stood on the sunny sidewalk and beamed at the frazzled

bartender.

Bree Mendez. Crimson-lipped viper of a woman.

His heart squeezed in his chest.

"I wasn't napping." She sounded furious, her cheeks flushing red at the suggestion. Like he hadn't just caught her first-hand, propped up against the faded brick wall, her mouth drooping open and soft snores coming from her mouth.

"Sure you weren't." Otis grinned, watching her eyes boil with rage. He had that effect on her.

Seeing Bree was exactly the distraction he'd needed this morning. Since he woke up, everything had gone wrong. His phone charger died. His car ran out of gas, forcing him to jog four miles to work. And when he'd arrived, sweating in the desert heat, he realized he forgot the key to the radio station.

Didn't matter. She was in front of him, which made today a Good Day. Even if she loathed the sight of him. Even if this was a crime scene.

"What's going on, Mendez?" He eyed the wrecked building behind her. "You finally snap?"

She huffed, but his eyes snagged on the claw marks gouged into the front door. That wasn't good. Twenty feet down the sidewalk, the Silver Bullet owner was huddled with a local cop. They muttered together, the cop making notes, and Otis didn't need heightened senses to catch the word *werewolves*.

Shit. This wasn't his pack's work—no way. He raised those wolves right, damn it, and though he was laid back by nature, he kept them in line.

This? This was criminal damage. Otis and his pack had no part in it.

"Why am I here?" he asked Bree, trying to sound pleasant. It came out wrong, even to his own ears. He sounded pissed off.

The bartender threw up her hands, then scrubbed at her face.

"I don't know," she muttered between her fingers. "I mean, I *do* know. Charlton thinks your wolves did this."

Otis figured as much, but he was glad to hear her say it. At least she didn't say she thought the wolves were guilty. At least she had the guts to tell him the truth.

"They didn't say so on the phone."

Bree muttered something into her hands. Something like *freaking cowards.* It buoyed him, puffing his chest up again. Gods, she was beautiful. Her dark hair was tied back in a messy bun, and strands had escaped to fall around her shoulders. More than anything, Otis wanted to reach out and wind a lock of her hair around his knuckle. To feel the silky soft strands against his rough skin; to watch the chestnut highlights catch the sunshine.

"Don't worry," he told her instead. "I won't tell them about your famous temper." He said it loud enough to carry down the sidewalk; to make the cop look over, face curious. Bree punched his shoulder hard, her face flaming, making him snort and stagger back. "Careful," Otis warned. "There are witnesses. People might talk."

"You piece of…" Bree broke off, strangling the air before massaging her temples. "I don't have claws," she muttered after a moment, dropping her hands. "Unlike some people, I couldn't have done this."

She was right. Otis sobered, sliding his phone out of his back pocket and shooting off a message to the pack group chat. He needed everyone's alibis for last night. He wanted everyone accounted for.

It didn't matter that he'd lived here for over ten years. Didn't matter that in all that time, Otis hadn't gotten so much as a parking ticket. He was the leader of the pack, which meant he was responsible. If one of his had done this, he'd go down for it too. And if Otis had a weakness, it was collecting waifs and strays. Anyone who needed somewhere to belong, he let in.

They didn't even have to be werewolves, truly. He ran Supernatural Airwaves like a pack all of its own. A pack of misfits and vampires and shifters and ghosts, and a cupid thrown in for good measure.

No. It didn't matter that Otis had never missed a town meeting. That he coached the high school track team. There was no such thing as a respectable werewolf, even in Boiling River. People were people, and people got scared of anybody different.

Even brave people like Bree.

* * *

The cop had the grace to look uncomfortable as Otis strode over. He walked with his shoulders back and down, his arms hanging loose by his sides. Like a neon sign hung over his head, saying: *innocent and nonthreatening!*

"Officer." Otis nodded, his nostrils flaring as he recognized a fellow shifter. Not a wolf, though; a big cat of some kind, judging by the scent.

His human face was familiar too—brown eyes and wild tawny hair. Handsome. Otis thought he'd maybe seen the cop before, laughing with Bree and her friends in the bar. Jealousy surged hot through his veins, but he tamped it down with the ease of practice.

Otis got jealous a lot around Bree. He prided himself on the fact no one noticed.

175

"Thank you for coming." The cop nodded to the Silver Bullet owner, the old windbag still ranting without pause, and walked away while the guy was mid-sentence. It made Otis like him just a tiny bit more. Just an inch. "We've received an accusation against your pack. That you're responsible for this damage. While many creatures could be responsible"—he threw a pointed look at the old biker—"we have to follow up on every lead."

"Understood." Otis didn't like it, but he could respect it. Sort of. "Is this an official interview? Do I need a lawyer?"

He didn't have one, but it sure sounded good. And the cop looked alarmed, shaking his head.

"No. These are informal questions."

Otis felt rather than heard Bree walk up behind him. She stopped at his elbow, a few inches from his side. Did she notice the way she always wound up standing beside him? The way she drifted toward him, pulled by an invisible current? Even when they were in a group, out with her friends and the vampire from his radio station, Bree always inched subconsciously nearer.

He wouldn't ask. If he knew anything about Bree, it was that once she noticed, she'd fight the urge to be close to him tooth and nail.

"The werewolves are tall." Bree spoke casually, but Otis could feel the tension radiating off her. It pissed her off that he was here, and not just because he annoyed her no end. She was *defensive* of him. Interesting. "All of them. They're all over six feet."

"So?" the bar owner barked, but the cop nodded, glancing at the door. Whatever she was saying, he was picking up. He gestured for Otis to stand next to the door, and Otis went gamely. He had nothing to hide.

"See?" Bree said, triumphant, and the cop nodded again. "Danny, come on. It wasn't him."

Danny. They were friendly, then. On a first name basis. Otis ground his teeth and forced the smile to stay on his face.

He would not be a territorial asshole. He would not be one of *those* men. Even if this shifter had broad shoulders and a chiselled face, and Bree called him *Danny.*

"Anyone want to clue me in?" Otis asked, voice pleasant. Bree huffed, but grabbed his forearm in her hands. His skin tingled under her warm, dry palms as she moved his hand in a slashing motion beside the door. He had to stoop to reach the bottom of the claw marks, his face bending closer to hers. She smelled like leather and dark cherries.

"See?" Bree sounded breathless. Either she was just as affected by him, or his arm was heavy. "You're too tall. Even shifted, this wouldn't be comfortable."

Otis took pity on her, straightening up and pulling his arm free. It was true—even on all fours as a wolf, he'd tower over these marks.

"He's the biggest one." The bar owner talked like Otis wasn't even here. The grizzly old bastard wouldn't even look at him. "The smaller ones could have done it."

Danny sighed, like he thought that was bullshit, but nodded again. Bree had proved nothing. Nothing, except that she secretly cared.

Otis leaned down to whisper in her ear as the other two men headed inside to inspect the damage.

"Don't worry, Mendez." Damn it, no matter how Otis tried, he couldn't help but needle her. "Your secret is safe with me."

"What secret?" She jerked her head away, crossing her arms

177

over her chest. A frown creased her forehead, and she glowered at the claw marks gouged through the wood.

"Oh, you know. The worst kept secret in all of Boiling River. That no matter how much you claim to hate me, you find me irresistible."

Bree scoffed and stomped inside, her thick leather boots crunching broken glass to powder. Otis grinned and followed after.

She could deny it as much as she liked, but he knew the truth. He felt it with every thump of his heart in his chest.

His fated mate couldn't ignore the pull for much longer.

Irresistible.

Check out Howl FM now!

About the Author

Tabby Monroe writes quirky & creepy paranormal romance.

When she's not writing, Tabby can be found baking, hiking, and befriending local cats.

She lives on the Welsh coast with her very own gorgeous vamp.

You can connect with me on:

🌐 https://www.tabbymonroe.com
📘 https://www.facebook.com/authortabbymonroe
✎ https://www.bookbub.com/authors/tabby-monroe